"If your brother isn't guilty,"

Wes said, "then someone else is."

Regina gasped. "And you think *I* might be?"

"I didn't say that."

"Well, you might as well have." She backed away from him. "And what about you, Mr. Blake? I understand you knew my brother's ex-wife."

"Yes. I knew her."

"Listen to us! We're talking in the past tense! We don't even know that anything has happened to her. She was rude and cruel and is probably on an island somewhere, just imagining what her supposed disappearance is doing to my brother!"

"You didn't like her, did you, Regina? And now she's missing...."

Dear Reader,

There's so much excitement going on this month that I hardly know where to begin. First of all, you've no doubt noticed that instead of the four Silhouette Intimate Moments novels you usually see, this month there are six. That increase—an increase you'll see every month from now on—is a direct result of your enthusiasm for this line, an enthusiasm you've demonstrated by your support right where it counts: at the bookstore or by your membership in our reader service. So from me—and all our authors—to you, *thank you!* And here's to the future, a future filled with more great reading here at Silhouette Intimate Moments.

And speaking of great reading, how about this month's author lineup? Heather Graham Pozzessere, Barbara Faith, Linda Turner, Rachel Lee and Peggy Webb, making her Intimate Moments debut. And I haven't even mentioned Linda Howard yet, but she's here, too, with *Mackenzie's Mission,* one of the most-requested books of all time. For all of you who asked, for all of you who've waited as eagerly as I have, here is Joe "Breed" Mackenzie's story. This is a man to die for (though not literally, of course), to sigh for, cry for and—since he's a pilot—fly for. And he's all yours as of now, so don't let him pass you by. And in honor of our increase to six books, and because Joe and some of the other heroes I have in store for you are so special, we've decided to inaugurate a special program as part of the line: American Heroes. Every month one especially strong and sexy hero is going to be highlighted for you within the line, and believe me, you won't want to miss his story!

Finally, I hope you've noticed our bold new cover design. We think it captures the sense of excitement that has always been the hallmark of Silhouette Intimate Moments, and I hope you do, too.

In the months to come, expect only the best from us. With authors like Kathleen Eagle, Emilie Richards, Dallas Schulze and Kathleen Korbel coming your way, how can the future be anything but bright?

Leslie Wainger
Senior Editor and Editorial Coordinator

MISTRESS

OF

MAGIC

Heather
Graham
Pozzessere

INTIMATE MOMENTS®

Published by Silhouette Books New York

America's Publisher of Contemporary Romance

SILHOUETTE BOOKS
300 East 42nd St., New York, N.Y. 10017

MISTRESS OF MAGIC

ISBN: 0-373-07450-6

First Silhouette Books printing September 1992

HEATHER GRAHAM POZZESSERE

considers herself lucky to live in Florida, where she can indulge her love of water sports, like swimming and boating, year-round. Her background includes stints as a model, actress and a bartender. She was once actually tied to the railroad tracks to garner publicity for the dinner theater where she was acting. Now she's a full-time wife, mother of five and, of course, a writer of historical and contemporary romances.

To Theresa Davant, Charlie and Stuart—
with lots of love

Chapter 1

Bump!

Large and green, shaded with yellow around the smiling mouth, the great eyes a brilliant, cornflower blue, the cuddly creature made of latex and foam came smacking lightly against the man as he absently turned away. The creature and the man turned to each other in surprise at the contact. Delighted laughter at the accidental interchange rose among the crowd.

The audience was ready to be delighted. It was fairly early, and though the day promised an intense heat, there was still a whisper of a breeze on the morning air. Beautifully manicured palms and hibiscus and crotons just bowed lightly to that breeze. Excitement and eagerness and even fun seemed to hang in the air like tangible things that could be swept up, grabbed and held tight.

The sudden, startling collision of the man and the latex monster seemed to add to it all.

The crowd laughed again. But between the man and the creature, there was a moment of silent surprise.

Then the man's face was split with a broad, handsome smile, and he bumped the creature in return—as if in a payback gesture. As if the creature had bumped into him on purpose.

The creature skittered away, then returned, then skittered away again, anxious, concerned, shy once again. The creature had a personality, one that was all her own, one that any child there knew and knew well.

"Pet her! Give her a pat on the nose, mister! Dierdre is really a nice monster, sir!" some young observer called out.

The man laughed. It was a nice laugh. The kind of laugh that somehow seemed to reach through all that latex and foam and padding and touch Reggie right against her spine, sending small electric tingles to race along it.

"A nice monster?" he said skeptically.

He had a nice voice, too. Deep, rich, very masculine. Reggie felt a peculiar trembling seize hold of her, just as if that voice could really touch her.

"Of course!" a little girl said.

"She'th thweet, she'th good, she'th wonderful!" added a stalwart tot who slurred out the words—he was missing his two front teeth.

"Then I'd better give her a pat, huh?" the man said.

"Yes, oh, yes!" the children all called out. A good sized crowd was gathering. Neither parents nor children seemed to mind that they would wind up running a little late to stand in their next line. They all seemed to enjoy the live drama—or comedy—that was taking place before them.

"A good monster. All right, nice monster!" he said, setting a hand on her latex nose.

Reggie felt another peculiar little trembling cascade through her. He wasn't even touching her. He was stroking latex. And still . . .

There could be definite advantages to wearing a dinosaur suit, she decided. Advantages she had certainly never imagined when Max had asked her to come out of the cave and play Dierdre for the first early morning crowd.

Really, Regina! she chided herself in dismayed silence. There had always been wonderful advantages to playing Dierdre Dinosaur!

For one, the children were wonderful. Reggie knew that a number of employees quickly tired of the heavy costumes and the multitude of children—big and little—who wanted to shake Dierdre's hand, stroke her synthetic cheek or just receive a big dinosaur hug.

Reggie had never minded. Of course, Dierdre Dinosaur was her invention, almost as much as the character was Max's creation. Dierdre had been their first. She was nearest and dearest to their hearts. Maybe Reggie felt something special for Dierdre.

Or maybe it was just the children. It was little faces alight with smiles. It was tiny hands, reaching out. Sometimes there were children in wheelchairs, children with terminal illnesses. Beautiful children with bright eyes and hope-filled faces, and then it was exceptionally wonderful to be Dierdre Dinosaur, just to see those extraordinary and very special smiles.

And, of course, there were times like this morning. Times when being Dierdre just turned out to be fun. Because the *very big* kids could sometimes be just as much fun as the little ones.

And as stunned as she might be with herself for such a volatile and startling reaction to a man, she would have to say that there was truly something especially fun about this particular big kid.

Well, he was *very* big, for one. Reggie was certain that he had to be over six two, probably closer to six three. He had a nice athletic build without being overly muscular, appealing broad shoulders, a narrow waist and trim hips. He wore his casual striped cotton tailored shirt with a pleasant ease, and seemed cool despite the rising heat.

And admittedly, he wore his tight jeans with an even greater appeal. The denim hugged his body quite nicely, and Reggie couldn't help but simply like the way the man was able to wear clothes.

And that, unfortunately, led her to wonder just what he looked like when he wasn't wearing clothing.

She groaned and reminded herself that she was a large, walking prehistoric animal-of-the-imagination and that she was out here to amuse children, not to think these thoughts that were causing her to blush beneath her mask. She wasn't like that. She never thought thoughts like that. Never. She always just had good, clean fun, enjoying her anonymity—

Oh, come now, Reggie! she told herself. This was still clean.

Nope. Not when she was using a dinosaur mask as a cover while discreetly studying the way he wore those jeans.

Heavens!

Look at his eyes, Reggie. Look at his eyes.

His face was even nicer than his body. He had a head of thick, sandy, fairly close-cropped hair. His face was the ruggedly handsome type, hard planed, lean, with a set of wide, hazel-gold eyes that gleamed sharply in contrast to the deep bronze hue of his skin. There was nothing soft or pretty about him. His were the rough-cut good looks that had given men like Clint Eastwood such a broad appeal. And still, despite the somewhat macho ruggedness of his appeal, he had a smile that could make her breath catch. Maybe because the full sensuality of his smile and that mischievous glitter in his eyes were somewhat in opposition to the severity of his face. Maybe he had been places and seen things. Maybe he'd weathered a lot.

But he seemed like the type who had come out of it all okay. With a sense of humor and a rich love of life still intact.

And maybe she was reading far too much into a stranger she was meeting as Dierdre Dinosaur, a stranger she would probably never meet in real life.

Well, it was fun. It was one way to pass the time. She received smiles from men in khaki shorts and women in halter tops and cutoff jeans all the time. She read the children's faces, and she even saw their lives back home in Des Moines or Charleston or whatever city they had traveled from to come here for their fun in the sun. She liked people, and she was a dreamer. It was what she and Max did for a living. The dreaming was the magic.

And still... Still, maybe she was imagining just a bit too much about this particular stranger.

Max had been telling her that she worked too hard, that she needed to get a life.

Mmm, but while he was in the midst of telling her that, he was also begging that she run out and be Dierdre again. With the employees beginning to leave since this new, ugly business had come up—

She didn't want to think about that! She didn't want to get angry or feel protective. She didn't want to feel hateful and furious, not when she was being Dierdre.

And that left . . .

The man. The man with his great, sexy smile and hazel-gold eyes. The man who was laughing now. He had withdrawn at first, like someone who quickly became wary. Why? Was he a cop? A government agent? Hmm.

He had actually seemed as if he was here on business, at first. As if the being accidentally bumped by a park creature had been an annoyance. She had seen that first look in his eyes. . . .

But this was an amusement park, a theme park. People came here to have fun. To see Dierdre Dinosaur, especially. And no one would be annoyed, unless it was a father who had stood in one too many long lines or a brother who had been dragged here by a younger sibling. . . .

This man was alone, or so it seemed.

And he had come around, she reminded herself. That annoyance had been in his glittering eyes for the very briefest of seconds. And then he had laughed and had joined right in the play, and the children were enjoying his impromptu performance just as much as they were enjoying the show being put on by the dinosaur.

Still smiling, he gave her another pat on the big dinosaur nose.

Dierdre, as shy and sweet as a dinosaur could be, bowed her head shyly. She half turned away.

"Oh, don't let him go! Don't let him go!" a little girl called out.

Reggie wasn't about to let him go. Actually, she decided, this could be really fun. As Miss Regina Delaney, she could certainly never flirt with a man like this.

But as Dierdre Dinosaur...

She turned quickly, using her three-pronged dinosaur hand to ruffle his close-cropped sandy blond hair. That stopped him. Stopped him quick. He turned back, his brows arched, a glimmer of high mischief in his eyes again. Even as he turned, she played the blushing dinosaur, hiding her face in her big dinosaur paws. She sneaked a peek. He was watching her, his head slightly cocked, his hands on his hips.

Good-looking fellow. Really good-looking fellow. Handsome smile, nice voice.

Not the type I ever get to meet as a human being! she said to herself. But I have him now...

And so she approached him again, setting her flopping arms around him and giving a little hug as she let her felt chin rest on his shoulder.

There was a pen in his pocket. Dexterous even in the costume—she had worn it often enough—Reggie slipped the pen from his shirt. Then she quickly sidled away again, shy. So shy.

A little boy chortled with laughter. "She's got your pen, mister!"

"You've got to give her a hug if you want it back!" another youngster warned.

"Hug a dinosaur?" he said in disbelief.

"Yes, yes!"

"Yeth!" the toothless child told him.

He shook his head in dramatic disbelief, then walked to the waiting dinosaur. Inside the costume, Reggie grinned at his whisper.

"There is a woman in there, I hope?"

Dierdre Dinosaur did not speak to the crowd. It was part of her magic, and that was the premise of the park—magic. The magic of the imagination, the magic of wonder. The magic of fantasy and the magic of belief.

"Please, have mercy, will you? You are a woman, right?" the man asked.

Dierdre Dinosaur gave him a slow nod. Then she realized that this stranger was a showman whether he had suspected it or not, for he threw his arms wide and enveloped her—massive costume and all—into a giant bear hug.

The children roared.

"Now, creature, my pen, please!" he commanded.

Dierdre gave him the pen. As he turned and started to walk away, she placed her three-toed hands together and set them palpitating over her heart. Once again, the children roared.

The man turned. Of course, by then, he was far too late. Dierdre was standing just as innocently as a creature of latex and foam could possibly stand.

"She wants a kiss goodbye!" a child called out.

"A big kith!" added the toothless one, passionately.

"You want me to kiss a monster?" the man asked.

"She's not a monster!"

"She's Dierdre Dinosaur!"

"And she loves you!"

"She loves everyone!"

"Hey, mister, don't you know? She's Dierdre Dinosaur!"

He knocked his palm against his head. "Of course! I know that! A kiss goodbye, huh?"

Through the big gauze eyes, Reggie could see his only slightly disconcerted expression as he walked toward her.

"You swear you're a woman, right?" he said again.

He was so damned uncomfortable. She should shake her head. Make him really sweat. But she didn't. She inclined her head instead.

"You've got me at one heck of a disadvantage, lady!"

She presented her cheek for a big kiss.

He sighed and planted a big kiss on it. "I don't kiss monsters for just anybody," he said.

She lifted a hand, indicating the gathering of children.

"You're right!" he said very softly. "Kids are just kind of worth it, huh?"

She started to nod, but he was wagging a finger at her in warning. "Still, lady, you've had me at a disadvantage. Remember that!"

Then he turned and walked away. The kids were laughing and calling.

Dierdre Dinosaur stood still for a moment, watching him.

Then Dierdre lifted her three-toed hand and beckoned to a little boy, and suddenly she was thronged with children.

Dierdre signed autographs awkwardly.

But the woman inside the dinosaur costume kept watching the man. She watched him as his broad shoulders and sandy head disappeared into the crowd.

The sun seemed to disappear behind a cloud, right along with him; the day had grown a little bit darker.

I don't even know him! she scolded herself. And there were so many serious things to worry about to-day.

But just like Dierdre, she felt as if her heart was palpitating hard against her breast.

And the day had, indeed, grown darker.

Fifteen minutes later she had managed to slip into the dinosaur cave from which she had come. As much as she loved playing Dierdre—and as well as the suits were crafted—the costumes could become unbearably hot in the kind of weather they were having, even though it was still early, not even summer yet. The rocky barriers of the cave gave way to one of the costume shops and to two dressing rooms, marked by some fun-loving employee as Dino Gals and Dino Guys. Dolly Duckbill—another of Reggie's favorites of their character creations—had come into the cave behind her. Already removing Dolly's headpiece was Dan Laredo, an old friend, a good friend, one who had been with her and Max from the beginning.

"Damnation, but it's going to be a scorcher!"

"Hot as Hades," Reggie agreed solemnly, "and watch that language with the kids."

Dan shrugged. He was dark, with a crinkled, good-humored face. He let out an expletive that seemed to let her know how he felt about the whole day—no children could hear him here.

She grimaced, but laughed at his exaggerated, pained expression. Then she sobered quickly. "Thanks for still being here, Dan."

"And playing a female dinosaur, at that!" he moaned.

"That should be the very least of your worries," she told him. Dan was a good friend, all right. And a long-time employee. He and she were both playing dinosaurs this morning because so many of the employees had already resigned.

It was going to be a long day for him. Just as it was going to be a long day for her. The *big* meeting was scheduled to take place at noon.

The fate of the park was at hand.

"How true," Dan said. Touchingly, he reached out a felt-clad hand. "Reggie, I will be here, you know. Till the very end."

Something hollow seemed to echo in her heart. Dan seemed to believe that there would be an *end*. Soon.

Well, everyone believed that. Everyone who heard the story. And the story was becoming very widespread. There were so many whispers going around. So much was rumor.

So much was truth.

And Max. Max was being made to pay for it all.

For the thousandth time, Reggie damned her ex-sister-in-law. Then she was sorry she did so, and she silently, quickly prayed that the woman might be all right.

But something was wrong. Dreadfully wrong. Her ex-sister-in-law was missing.

Nothing had ever been enough for the woman. Nothing had ever been right. She and Max had seemed mismatched from the start. And Reggie had stayed away, determined never to let Max know her feelings. Never to be even the ghost of a note of discord between them. But then things had exploded on their own, the messy, sticky divorce had come about and now...

And now the woman was missing, and the police thought she was dead.

And they were making everyone think Max was responsible.

And while the rumors surfaced, the resignations began to pour in. Financial backers were pulling out. The park was in the midst of a crisis. Max's silent partner was planning on making an appearance at the meeting, Reggie had heard, and she was nervous. She had never met W. D. Blake, but she could picture him—a stuffy old millionaire, ready to pull the curtains on Max.

But it wasn't true. Max Delaney would never murder anyone. He might have been furious. He might have hated his ex-wife. And he might have put his fist through a wall, but he would never, never hurt a woman. Reggie knew her brother.

He hadn't killed anyone. Until her dying day, Reggie would swear that Max had had nothing to do with the woman's disappearance.

But that might not matter, not so far as the park mattered. The park might die anyway, just like Dan seemed to think.

"Reggie—" Dan began.

But she didn't want to talk about it. She'd have to face it sooner or later. Sooner. The meeting would come soon enough. And for now, the depression was wearing down on her already.

Any more misery was going to have to wait!

"You were a wonderful Dolly Duckbill!" she told him cheerfully. "And I'm roasting! Scoot. I'll see you later." She gave him a shove toward the Dino Guys room and started for the Dino Gals. But as she started walking, she realized that there was a small tear along one of her felt-striped arms. She took an automatic turn toward the costume shop. Once inside the empty large room, she closed the door, then walked to one of the small sewing cabinets and set Dierdre's head down while she rummaged in a drawer for a needle and thread.

She could leave the costume for later; she could also just go ahead and mend it now. It suddenly seemed important that she mend it. She and Max were going to have to save money. Despite the fact that it was summer, that the schools were out, people weren't flocking here the way they had last year.

How could they? Speculation was out that Max Delaney might have murdered his ex-wife.

She couldn't quite fix the tear with the costume on. She looked around, but only costumes and dinosaur eyes stared back at her. Impatient, she wriggled out of the costume and stood barefoot in her bra and underwear, the costume heavy in her hands. Brows knit, she tried to concentrate on the tear in the costume and not on the very serious issues that were plaguing her life.

She was good and quick with a needle. When she and Max had started out, they had made all their creatures by themselves, by hand. She had learned to sew, cut and baste, and she had done it all lovingly. It had been wonderful to see these creatures spring forth from their imaginations to become real before their eyes.

There was the slight sound of a movement—a shuffle?—something, and Reggie felt as if the hair on the back of her neck pricked up. She stuck her finger with her needle, and automatically issued a sharp, "Ouch!" Fool! If someone was spying on her, she needed to be silent!

There might be a murderer loose in the park, she thought suddenly. Since Max was *supposed* to be the murderer, and she knew that Max was innocent, then . . .

The costume shop was off limits to anyone but certain employees. In fact, once she had been inside, once that door had closed behind her, anyone would have needed a key to follow her.

"Who's there?" she called out, hoping to sound authoritative. But her voice quavered.

"It's all right," came a voice in reply.

She froze. Not *a* voice. *His* voice. The man—the stranger from the crowd.

For a moment, she didn't see him. Then she saw him standing between a costume of Tyrannosaurus Tex and one of the large industrial sewing machines. If she had turned before, she would have seen him.

"You!" she whispered.

What was he doing there? He must have been in the back when she had arrived. He had come up on her silently. He had been in the costume shop just as if he belonged there. As if he had every right to be there.

And he was serious once again. Very serious. Not even a hint of a smile touched the taut, grim contours of his mouth. The hard, almost world-weary look was in his eyes. Gold and hard, they stared at her, judging her.

He obviously hadn't expected her to be here.

But he was the stranger! She was the one dressed up as Dierdre Dinosaur—No. She *had* been dressed as Dierdre Dinosaur. Now she was standing here barefoot in crimson bikini panties and a lace-frothed bra.

Absurdly, she was glad that she had drawn out matching underwear that morning.

Absurd, indeed! This man had no right to be here! And he certainly had no right to stare at her so, his handsome face so cold and hard....

But then the look was suddenly gone. His hands were on his hips and a sizzle was in his eyes as he looked her up and down. A grin tugged at his lower lip.

"You *are* a woman," he said softly.

Softly, and still the voice was a haunting one. So masculine. Now that she was practically naked, it seemed to touch her all the more, starting at the nape of her neck and stroking the length of her spine. Touch upon touch. A rasp of rough velvet ...

"What in God's name are you doing in here!" she managed to rasp out suddenly.

His brow arched high. He was silent for a beat, and she hurried on.

"You've no right to be in here! This is off-limits to anyone but employees. You have to get out. Now! Right now!" she emphasized indignantly.

If she had been dressed—if she hadn't felt his eyes, and his voice, so keenly—would she have been so upset? She didn't know, and she didn't get a chance to know.

Because he wasn't in a big hurry to leave. He was sauntering slowly toward her, and he seemed amused. Tremendously amused.

Suddenly he stood right in front of her. Only the costume held awkwardly in her hands stood between him and her near-naked form. He lifted a hand from his hip. A finger wagged just beneath her nose. "You were enjoying yourself out there, weren't you? Tousling the hair, getting me to kiss a latex cheek and so on."

She pulled the costume close to her chest with what she hoped was a great deal of dignity. "I was trying to entertain the children—"

"And I was at the disadvantage. I couldn't see the face. Or the form."

Her eyes narrowed on his hazel ones. "Well, you have seen both now. And you are not supposed to be in here! Now, if you don't leave quickly, I'll—"

"You'll what? Call the dino police?" he asked lightly.

Her gaze sizzled. "We do have park security," she warned steadily. He was behaving atrociously! He should be apologizing and hurrying out. He should be making up some sort of excuse for being where he shouldn't be, in a place that was clearly marked out-of-bounds to park guests!

He was still staring at her.

"If you don't—" she began.

"Indeed, you are a woman!" he murmured. There was amusement in his voice. It was annoying.

It also caused a whole new wave of tremors. The tone of his voice was still sexy. Dangerous, in a way.

Irritating.

And still . . . Sexy. Just like the way he watched her.

"Every inch a woman." His eyes didn't leave hers, but she knew he was remembering everything he had seen when his eyes had traveled over the length of her.

The finger wagging beneath her chin suddenly touched it. She felt as if his touch burned and seared her. As if she would feel it forever— Why was she letting him touch her?

She didn't really think or wonder long, because as quickly as that touch had come, it was gone.

"I told you that *I* would have an advantage," he said softly. "I hadn't planned this, but . . ."

Now his eyes did roam the length of her. "You are at the disadvantage. And it's been my most sincere pleasure."

Her face reddened to crimson despite herself. Her voice lowered to a furious whisper.

"If you don't—"

"I'm going," he told her. But he still wasn't in a hurry. He inclined his sandy head slightly. His mouth was still curled into a small grin of amusement. He stepped slowly around her. She turned, her eyes following him.

He walked to the door, saluted her and disappeared beyond it.

"Damn him!" she exploded.

The air-conditioning suddenly seemed to wash over her hot flesh. She shivered and flushed from head to toe.

And only then did she realize that she still had no explanation for the man being in the costume shop— or any idea of how he had come to be in it.

Chapter 2

The dinosaur was a woman.

All woman—every lush, entrancing curve of her.

Wes Blake couldn't quite help smiling as he left the costume shop behind and headed through the growing crowds for one of the buildings across the crowded main Dino Street of the park. Above the main Dino Store and Dierdre Dress Shop were a number of small offices. Max Delaney had seen to it that Wes had been given some space here, next to Max's office and that of his sister, Regina.

Regina. Reggie. He'd heard so much about her over the years from Max. But still, he hadn't expected the woman he had just met.

He slipped around the stucco cave walls of the shop to the private entrance and rode a small elevator to the top floor. He walked down a handsomely carpeted hallway, past Miss Wainwright's desk—saluting the dragon lady promptly—and onward to his own office. There was a large desk in the center of the room and a sleep sofa opposite it, a bath and dressing room to the side, shelves of glasses for sodas and drinks, and a small refrigerator to supply whatever his whim might be. In a glass case was an old puppet—maybe twenty-five years old by now, one of the very first Dierdre Dinosaurs. It had been crafted by very young hands and signed on the bottom of a foot by Max and Regina Delaney.

He sat back in the comfortable swivel chair behind the desk. He'd like a Scotch. His head was pounding, but the meeting was coming up.

Hell, he'd have a Scotch anyway. One wasn't going to change the way he saw the world.

He poured himself a drink, then sat back in the chair again, resting his feet on the desk as he sipped the fiery liquid. It was good Scotch.

Max would have seen to it that it was the best.

He'd known Max for over twelve years now. Ever since they had entered the service as scared young kids, volunteers who were suddenly wondering just what they had volunteered for.

They had found out together, serving three years in the same company. They had been a rough three years, spent mostly in Central American jungles.

Max Delaney had broken up much of the tedium and the misery and the heat. Wes had learned that slowly. Little by little, he would notice that children flocked around their tents. Max Delaney didn't care how dirty they were, or how many.

He could make a puppet out of anything. Torn socks, paper bags. And he created great characters for the children. When Wes first commented on the ingenuity of his creations, Max would always tell him, "Oh, these are nothing. You should see what I can do with Reggie." And he would grimace. "Reggie can sing. I tend to sound like a dying swan." Then Max learned that Reggie was studying, she had earned a scholarship to a prestigious arts school. "I can help her a little with what I make here," Max had told him. "And then, when I get out, I'll have Uncle Sam's help to get through school myself. But if you ever meet Reggie, remember that she thinks I'm here because I want to be here, all right?"

Sure, if he ever met Reggie, he'd lie.

And he understood a lot about Max. Delaney didn't talk much about the past, but Wes knew that he and his sister had grown up being passed from relative to relative.

He knew a lot about that kind of status, too. He hadn't the faintest idea who the Blake who had fathered him had been; his mother had died on a sidewalk in New York when he had been ten, and he had just sat down next to her and cried.

That had been the last time he could remember crying. Real tears. He hadn't even been able to shed them again when he had lost Shelley years later.

Of course, he hadn't known about Shelley then. Nor had he met Reggie, not then. Somehow he and Max managed to stay in the dangerous jungles, hoping they would get home. But during those days, just as Wes learned that Max had his artistic talents, Max commented that Wes had a nose for gathering intelligence. Their superiors noticed it, too.

When their enlisted period was up, Wes went on to officers' training school. Max left the army to return to the States and his sister.

"You're going to make a good living out of those puppets," Wes told him.

"And you're going to survive wherever you go," Max said in return, as they clasped hands. "If I ever need someone in my corner, I'll be calling on you."

They had seen each other five years later in San Francisco. Max had just gotten a series on public television for his puppets. The idea for the theme park had come to him, and he had already drawn up a multitude of plans.

"I can start small," he had told Wes excitedly. "Reggie can be half of the entertainment!" he had added with a laugh. "And if the television series is a go, I'll be able to get the backing."

Wes had been amazed at how ready Max was to start.

And he could help.

Just two months before his meeting with Max, he had been called by a lawyer's office in New York City.

His grandfather had died.

He hadn't known he'd had a grandfather. The man hadn't bothered to offer a nickel for his mother to receive a pauper's plain coffin, much less show up for the funeral! He'd tried to feel something; he hadn't been able to.

But he'd suddenly inherited an indecent sum of money, and he wasn't sure what he wanted to do with it.

He'd bought his mother the most beautiful, gaudy marble angel he could find. And he'd offered the rest of it to Max.

Max hadn't been able to believe his good fortune. At first he hadn't been willing to accept the money. "I mean to sell stocks—"

"And you'll still have to sell stocks. But maybe what I've got can hurry things along."

"But, Wes—"

"Max, I've never met a man who was a better investment."

He had meant it then, and he meant it now. Max Delaney hadn't killed anyone. And he wasn't here now because he was worried about his investment or because he had any questions whatsoever about Max.

He was here to prove Max was innocent.

It seemed he would have some passionate help in that direction.

Reggie.

He smiled suddenly, even if the smile was a little grim. Max Delaney was a handsome man, and Wes had heard that Regina resembled her brother. Somehow, though, he'd just never been able to see Max's sharp green eyes and jet dark hair on a woman.

Now...now he could see them. Easily. Regina Delaney was beautiful. Exotic even, with her slightly tilted, brilliant eyes, soft ivory complexion and long, pitch dark hair. Where Max's chin was squared, hers was a gamin's, delicate, just slightly pointed, for her face was heart-shaped, her eyes were large and lustrous, and her mouth...

Hmm. Her mouth was made for kissing. He'd never thought that way about a woman's mouth before. But hers was. Fully defined, rich, generous—she had beautiful lips.

She liked to play games.

But only when the ball was in her court.

He lifted his feet suddenly from his desk, glancing at the watch on his left wrist. The meeting was just minutes away and he wanted to grab a quick shower and change.

He realized suddenly that his heart was pounding quickly. He felt warm, anxious. Excited. The adrenaline was ripping through his system. Over the meeting?

He didn't think so. He paused, smiling slowly. Could it be the furious Miss Regina Delaney? Could this thing be a raw—dare he think it?—desire?

Yes. For his best friend's sister.

Well, she was no child. And she had started the game.

Well, Miss Delaney, the game is about to continue. If she was displeased with him at the moment, she was going to be even more displeased when she discovered who he was.

None of that really mattered, he reminded himself sternly. Max mattered. The truth mattered.

But Regina was irrefutably entangled with Max.

And so, though she might not realize it yet, he thought grimly, Reggie Delaney was irrefutably entangled with him now, too. With that thought firmly in place, he hurried in for a shower.

To his aggravation, he discovered that it needed to be a cold one. Very cold.

Because no matter how hard he tried to think of Max, he kept picturing Max's sister as she had stood there in the costume shop, curves and limbs so elegantly, beautifully... sensually displayed.

He groaned aloud and turned off the hot water altogether.

The main offices for Dierdre's DinoLand were atop the large stucco and brick cave through which guests entered the park. There were large picture windows through which the executives, employees and whomever else happened to enter into such sacred company ground could observe guests arriving, being greeted and entering the park. In the center of the offices was a large boardroom, and it was here that Regina hurried as soon as she had repaired the Dierdre costume and changed into her street clothing.

Long after the man with the golden eyes had swept past her to exit the costume shop, she had still felt as if he was with her. She had still felt those eyes on her, seen in her mind's eye the curve of his smile.

The air had remained charged with his energy, and she had spent long moments looking after him, wondering about him. She'd wanted to call him back. To give him a good shaking.

She wanted to know how the hell he had gotten into the costume shop.

And most of all, she felt a peculiar aching, wondering if she'd ever see him again.

Then she'd been angry with herself. Still, it wasn't so bad that she should have an intense interest in such a brazen stranger. But the nerve of the man, appearing in the shop, then behaving as if he had every right to be there! That was obviously why she'd stared after him. She'd been angry. Really angry. She'd best not see him again. She'd call security for certain.

And then she'd finally managed to dress, her flesh still feeling as if it was on fire.

Max! She reminded herself. Max! The business meeting. How on earth could she be worrying about anyone else when Max was in such grave difficulty?

She had chosen a very businesslike red suit with a red and white striped tailored blouse beneath it. She wasn't sure at first why she had chosen the red or the shirt, but when she thought about it, she realized she had certainly been preparing for battle. In her artistic pursuits she had learned that red was a bold color. And she did intend to brazen her way through the meeting!

And the tailoring of her dress? Easy. The rest of the execs were men. She was going to be playing with the big boys. She wanted to be taken seriously. She was out to defend Max.

Even as she hurried along the hallway to reach the meeting room, she reminded herself that Max didn't exactly want to be defended, and certainly not by his sister. Little sister, she thought ruefully.

They were twins, but she had been born five minutes after Max. He had never let her forget those few minutes. He had always tried to be the big brother. They had grown up squabbling, but they had grown up best friends. Both had their moments of yearning for independence and had a great deal of respect for the other's freedom and space.

But in times of crisis, no siblings could be closer.

Her fingers were trembling slightly as she set them on the door leading to the board of directors' chamber. Be still! she commanded them. She twisted the doorknob and entered the room. The first person she saw was Max, standing by one of the windows, looking at the park.

A startling, almost overwhelming feeling of warmth filled her as she watched her brother, for the moment unobserved in return. Max loved children. He loved them of all ages, but he especially loved small children. Children when they were impressionable—children at an age when they could so easily be lost and hurt.

Children at the age she and Max had been when they had lost their parents, when they had first learned the shuffling from airport to airport, from relative to relative.

That age when it was so necessary to believe in dreams and magic!

Her brother was a handsome man. Tall and dark and very serious at this moment, reflective. He stood in a dark suit, his hands clasped lightly behind his back, his classically chiseled features arresting in the soft, artificial light of the room. There was so much for him to lose at this moment!

An intense feeling of dislike for Daphne, Max's ex-wife, came rushing swiftly down on Reggie, and then a breathless sensation filled her and she was silently praying. No, God, I didn't mean it. Make Daphne be all right, please, let her be all right.

But she didn't think Daphne was all right. The signs were too disturbing. And so she just couldn't help but pray that, no matter what Daphne's situation, it wouldn't ruin this magic Max had created. Yes, this was business! And yes, she and Max made a nice living off the park. But it was more than that. They opened their doors to so many foundations!

To orphans, to the sick. To the weary and the lost. Max never forgot the need for a little bit of fantasy and magic in every life.

Her brother turned to her suddenly. Intuitively, he had known that she was there. He tried to smile quickly, reassuringly. She knew the smile was a front, but she offered him a bold one in return.

"Regina!" She hadn't taken a step toward Max before she heard her name spoken softly. She felt a faint whisper of unease come rushing along her spine.

Rick. Rick Player. He was the fourth largest stockholder in the corporation and held a position on the board. Rick came from money. Big money. He'd spent his life playing polo and golf and letting his money make more money. He was blue-eyed, blond and suntanned to perfection, suave, charming....

And slimy. In all the years she had known him, Reggie had never felt comfortable with him. There was something licentious, so it seemed, beneath every word he said. She never liked the way he accidentally touched her whenever they spoke. Brushed by her. Came too close.

"Rick," she said quietly. It wasn't time to go to battle against Rick. Nor did she want Max to see just how uncomfortable Rick made her.

Max wouldn't understand that she, too, didn't need defending. Rick wasn't particularly after her in his slimy way—Rick was after any female he came across.

Rick had been after Daphne. Continually.

But Daphne hadn't minded. She had liked adulation, and she had liked to collect men. Whenever one seemed smitten by her, she would make sure Max realized he had something other men coveted.

"Reggie," he said, blue eyes hooded by his blond lashes as his gaze swept her up and down. "You look wonderful. Wonderful. Of course you always do, but red seems to be your color." He lifted a hand, casually brushing his fingers over the hair at the side of her head, hair she had drawn up in a tight, neat twist. "Your hair looks as ebony as a raven's wing against the red, Reggie. It's beautiful."

She withdrew slightly. "Thank you, Rick."

"It's been too long since I've seen you, Reggie. I'm still waiting for you to run out of excuses for that dinner date I've been wanting. When did we meet last?"

"I believe it was the last stockholders' meeting," Reggie murmured, trying to look beyond him. Dinner? The fate of the entire park was up for grabs today and Rick was thinking about dinner dates?

"Yes, that was it. I asked you to dinner then, and you politely declined, telling me that you still weren't up to it after—after Caleb's accident. Of course, it had been over a year since the accident then. I hope you won't still refuse me on those grounds!"

Refuse him? She wasn't really hearing him at the moment. She was trying to sort through the rest of the men in the room. Talking together in the far corner were Niles Sherman and Jesse Brant. Jesse was president of the company, a septuagenarian with wonderfully dignified posture, steel gray eyes and a thick head of snow-white hair. He was a veteran of many amusement parks and knew his management well. Niles held the positions of treasurer and press liaison officer. Like Jesse, he had been around for many years. Niles had worked with the biggest and the best in the field of entertainment complexes; he had come to work for Max because he'd had so much belief in Max's commitment to his work. Niles didn't need to work; he did so because, like Max, he was a believer in magic.

But Niles, like Jesse, looked grave today.

Only Rick seemed to be unaware of the tension in the room. Rick and...

In the far corner of the room, in the shadows created by the artificial light centered on the polished oak table, stood the last of the board members.

Max's silent partner, Reggie thought. The man with the real money behind the enterprise. Silent no more, it seemed.

She squinted imperceptibly, trying to see him, wishing that she had given the business part of this enterprise more attention in the past. But that wouldn't have mattered. Max's main backer had never put in an appearance before.

She couldn't see him. The light was too bright in the center of the room, too muted where he stood. She imagined him to be a septuagenarian, like Jesse. Dignified like Jesse, or with a shining, bald pate like Niles. His name was Wesley Blake, that was about all she really knew. Max had felt obliged to reach him immediately, the moment he had been advised that Daphne was missing—and that the fallout from it was going to fall on him.

But Wesley Blake had already known. He had told Max he was making his travel arrangements already.

Please, please let him be like Jesse or Niles! Reggie thought. Both of the older men knew Max and believed in him. If Wesley Blake was the same...

"Well, Reggie?"

"What?"

She drew her focus to Rick Player with a polite smile.

"Dinner—how about dinner tonight?" He lowered his voice. "Maybe between the two of us, we can figure a way out of this for old Max. Terrible thing, isn't it, this Daphne business. Terrible, terrible."

She felt a smile curl her lip. "You should know, Rick. You did seem fond of Daphne! And naturally, I assume you must be very worried."

His playboy smile faded a little, despite the innocence of her gaze. "As yet, we're not even sure that there is anything to be worried about."

"Right. But then . . . there are rumors."

"Poor Max."

"My brother is innocent."

"Of course, of course. Innocent of what?"

"Of any wrongdoing," Reggie insisted coolly.

The man in the shadows was moving toward Max. Reggie tried to get a look at him.

Rick Player blocked her way.

"Reggie, how about dinner? You haven't answered me yet."

"I've already made—" she began, but broke off, inhaling a gasp of astonishment. She had seen him at last. He had crossed the room; he had reached her brother. He had set a hand lightly on Max's arm and was speaking to him softly.

The partner. The silent partner. The man who was to be silent no longer.

He was no septuagenarian. He was neither bald, nor gray, silver nor white-haired.

He was a young man, midthirtyish. Despite the power in the room, despite all these people who knew what they were doing, who knew what they were up against, who were leaders in this field, there was a look about him that seemed to state he would be the one to take charge here.

He was no stranger.

He was Dierdre Dinosaur's playmate. The man whose hair she had tousled. The man she had teased. The man in the park. The man who had startled her in the costume shop and stared at her so intently.

The man who had seemed to find every advantage...

She felt her cheeks redden. Wesley Blake was coming toward her.

Chapter 3

"Reggie! Reggie!"

Rick Player was talking to her again. She couldn't breathe. She couldn't speak. Wesley's eyes were on her as he and Max walked toward her. He had changed for the meeting, too. He wore a lightweight summer suit, handsomely tailored, one that emphasized his broad shoulders and trim waist. The suit gave him an air of civilization that seemed foreign to the gold glimmer of his eyes, to the rugged appeal of his features.

No, it didn't seem to give him an air of civilization. It gave him the air of a very sleek tiger, velvet to touch—until the claws came jutting from soft fur and the mouth opened in a roar to display the deadly teeth. A wolf in sheep's clothing. He was certainly a dangerous man—and he didn't give a damn if anyone knew it.

Nor did he give a damn about what she might have to say about him. He was standing before her with Max at his side, and he was staring straight at her. Obviously, he didn't care if she mentioned that they had met—or how—to her brother or anyone else.

There was the slightest curl of amusement to his lip, as if he dared her to say whatever she chose to say.

Anger churned inside her.

And that heat. That same awful heat. Sweeping over her flesh as if she was nearly naked again, as if she wasn't dressed in the conservative, encompassing red suit. And she experienced the disturbing thought that this man might make her feel naked no matter what she was wearing, and that it would go far beyond the obvious because he looked beyond the flesh and into the soul.

She gritted her teeth. The air seemed to be charged between them. Maybe Rick Player was aware of it. Max wasn't. But Max had big things on his mind.

"Reggie, I don't think you and Wes have ever met. Of course, you've heard me talk about him often enough. Wes, the real creative genius here, my sister, Regina. Regina, Wesley Blake. Wes, you've met Rick Player, right?"

"Yes." That voice again. Deep. Rich. And the little thrills went dancing up and down her spine.

And still she stared at the man coolly. "We've met," Reggie said smoothly, her eyes on his as she gave the assurance to her brother. "Mr. Blake neglected to tell me who he was, but then, perhaps, he didn't know who I was."

His grin suddenly deepened. It was disarming. "I didn't know right away. It's hard to discern much about a woman when she's wearing a large dinosaur costume. But afterward..." His voice trailed with just the slightest insinuation. "I knew. In an entirely feminine way, Miss Delaney, you have quite a resemblance to your brother."

"We're twins," Max reminded him with a shrug. "Quite a bit alike."

"Yes and no," Wesley Blake said.

Max heard nothing amiss. Rick Player did. He took a step closer to Reggie. "Dinner?" he persisted, almost beneath his breath.

Max frowned. No matter what Reggie said, he wouldn't interfere—not here, not now. But he was unhappy and uncomfortable and didn't want her having dinner with Rick Player anytime, anywhere.

Reggie wasn't sure how she was going to opt out of it—and keep Rick on her brother's side for the meeting to come. Max, of course, would be furious if he sensed that she would consider dinner with this man in any effort on his behalf. She was in a bind.

"Dinner?" Wesley Blake echoed. His eyes were hard on hers. "But you already promised that meal to me, Miss Delaney."

She wasn't sure if she wanted to slap him—or give him a big kiss on the cheek. He had come very intuitively into the situation.

She didn't want to appreciate a single thing this man might be doing for her, but what choice did she have at the moment?

She was staring at him. She had to say something quickly. Rick Player was many things, but stupid wasn't among them. If she didn't say something fast...

"Oh, did you two make dinner plans already?" Max asked. "How interesting!"

"Yes, how very interesting!" Rick said, his white smile in place, his voice low and irritated. "Especially when you hadn't really met. I admit, I am confused."

Regina offered him a broad smile and inhaled deeply, ready to speak.

She didn't need to.

"It was very interesting, indeed," Blake said lightly, addressing Rick Player, but his gaze casually falling upon Reggie. "I happened to be walking through the park when I came across a dinosaur."

"Oh, yeah. And these creatures are captivating, right?" Rick said.

"I always thought so," Max supplied blandly. Wes cast him a quick glance of amusement. His lip curled further. The golden eyes glittered.

Indeed, he was like a tiger. With prey all lined up, right in front of him!

Max knew damned well that she and Wes had made no dinner arrangements. Blake had picked up on her brother's annoyance with Rick Player. They did know each other well. It was almost as if they shared a bond.

Like she had always shared with her brother.

An inward groan seized her. Oh, come! She wasn't going to be jealous of a friendship between the two!

"I never could resist a dinosaur myself," Wesley said.

"Right. Because you can see those feminine curves right off the bat, eh?" Rick said. He was growing more and more annoyed. Obviously, things were not proceeding to his liking. Though he apparently knew that the others were finding an amusement at his expense, it didn't occur to him that his own personality might have brought it about.

Blake stared at him. "It was amazing. I felt this startling attraction to a dinosaur. But then, of course, the lady did have an advantage over me. But later, the tables were turned. I discovered that my dinosaur had more than a wonderful personality. And so I decided that dinner just had to be on the agenda."

Rick Player looked straight at Reggie. He smiled, but it wasn't a friendly smile. "And you said yes, just like that. My. My, my."

"I never gave her a chance to say yes or no."

"So then what about me?" Rick asked pointedly.

Well, this seemed like a wretched place between a rock and hard wall, Reggie decided. If she told Rick the truth—that she'd rather dine with a dozen mite-infested rodents than with him, he'd surely fight them tooth and nail.

He might still do so anyway.

And then there was Wesley Blake, who made her shiver each time he spoke. Whom she wanted to strangle. Who made her feel so, hot and burning. And who had, indeed, turned the tables and taken every advantage.

Still, he didn't really expect her to go to dinner. He was playing this all out strictly because he knew how her brother felt about Rick Player.

"I am sorry, Rick." She offered Wes Blake a fetching—if false—and enthusiastic smile. "I'm afraid that Mr. Blake did take me off guard!"

"And you said yes?"

"I simply can't wait to have dinner with him."

Wesley Blake caught hold of her hand. The rough touch of his callused palm and fingers sent electric chills cascading into her. The cold became hot and seemed to scald her, inside and out. And like that fire, his eyes, too, seemed to burn inside her when they caught her own.

"It is a promise, Regina, right?"

Rick was watching her intensely. She tried not to snatch her hand away.

"A promise," she murmured a little breathlessly.

"Well, that's all set!" Max said.

All set? But it wasn't real! "I may be working this evening—" Reggie began.

"And then again, after this meeting, there may be no need for anyone to be working here, right?" Rick said politely.

Wes Blake shifted. Just slightly. "Last I heard," he said softly, "I'm still the majority stockholder."

"But this is a board meeting. And we'll be voting on a number of things," Rick said.

"And we should get to it, right?" Max said. He backed away from their foursome to address Jesse and Niles, as well. "Coffee and water are on the table. Let's get to this, shall we?"

Reggie felt herself suddenly propelled along. Then she was being seated in one of the massive leather chairs that surrounded the highly polished table.

Wesley Blake was at one end of it, next to her. Her brother was at the other end. Rick Player was on the other side of her, and Niles and Jesse were across the table.

"Who wants to start?" Max asked. Long moments of silence followed his words. "Come on, now. I called this meeting because I'm aware of the things being written in the papers, and because I know how concerned you all are.''

Rick Player cleared his throat, leaning forward. ''All right, let's lay it all right on the table. You're right, Max. We are concerned.'' He waved a well-manicured hand in the air. ''This place is based on fantasy. On family values. Max, how many parents are going to bring their children to a park whose creator is being accused of murder?''

Though it was true and a good point, Reggie didn't care. She jolted forward. ''We don't even know that there *has* been a murder, and *if* there has, Max didn't commit it,'' she stated flatly.

''Reggie, Reggie!'' Rick murmured, sorrowfully shaking his head at her. In that one glance he seemed to tell her that things might have gone differently—might have!—if she had agreed to dinner. And whatever else might have come with that singular meal. But she had scorned him one time too many, and she—and Max—were going to pay. ''Reggie, it doesn't matter whether Max is guilty or not. Heck, if he had throttled Daphne, not many men would really blame him!''

''And you would know, right?'' Reggie suggested sweetly.

Rick slammed a hand on the table. ''Regina, there was no call for that!''

''And Max is innocent!''

''Regina!'' Max said sharply, entering into the fray. She clenched her teeth. Max didn't like being defended by his sister. He was a big boy, one who liked to go to battle for himself. Or maybe it was just that he didn't want his sister waging war. Perhaps he would accept a little battle assistance from elsewhere.

But Wesley Blake was sitting at the end of the table in silence. His hands were folded, resting idly in his lap. His keen hazel eyes seemed almost shielded by the fall of sandy lashes. Was he intensely paying attention? Or was he bored silly? It was impossible to tell.

It seemed that he intended to let Max sink or swim on his own.

"Let's all simmer down here a little bit," Niles suggested in a gentle, weary manner as he turned to Max. "This is a grave concern. Once all this hits the papers as more than speculation—well, then, we will be in trouble."

"Unless we get Max out of it quickly," Jesse suggested unhappily. "Max could sell his shares and step aside for the time being. If we broadcast that as clearly and loudly as we can, let the papers and the media get hold of it, we might come out with our heads above water."

"Have Max sell out!" Reggie exclaimed, astounded.

"It wouldn't hurt to have Reggie do the same thing," Rick said. "After all, their name is the same. It's well known that they're twins. The taint of one..."

"It wouldn't necessarily have to be forever. Just until this blows over," Jesse suggested mildly.

"Until Daphne—is found. One way or the other," Niles said.

"Is that what you want?" Max asked his older advisers flatly.

Niles shook his head slowly. "No, it's not what I want, Max—"

"It's Max's park!" Reggie exclaimed. She just couldn't believe what she was hearing.

"It's *our* park," Max said softly to her. "Yours and mine, because we created it in our hearts. But it belongs to everyone here, too, and to the others out there who have invested in us, Reggie."

"It's just that Max's leaving may be a solution," Jesse said.

"We do want to save the park, right?" Rick said. He looked like the cat who had swallowed the canary. Whole.

Niles suddenly turned to the man at the end of the table. "Mr. Blake, you're going to be the deciding factor here. What do you think?"

Blake finally looked up, his hazel eyes burning. "Well," he drawled softly. "The last I heard, a man was innocent until he was proven guilty."

"Yes, Blake," Rick Player said impatiently. "We're all in sympathy with Max—"

"I didn't say that I was in sympathy," Wes said. His voice was still soft. Somehow, it managed to crack like a whip, and everyone was silent. And waiting. "I think you're all misjudging our fellow Americans. Many of them will also believe that a man is innocent until proven guilty. Hell, Max hasn't even been officially accused of anything yet. We're jumping the gun here, incredibly."

"Yes," Rick said, impatient once again. "Because these things take time. We need to get rid of all association with Max before—"

Wes shook his head. "Max and Regina are the foundations of this park. They are the creative element, and more than that. Maybe much more than you can understand, sir. If they're gone, the way I see, you'll have nothing but a shell of a park to begin with. The magic will be gone. And if that happens, then yes, we'll be in serious trouble.''

Jesse's face crinkled into a broad smile. "That's right! That's what so many fail to see. You have to have the magic!''

Rick groaned. He'd had both Jesse and Niles on his side. And now he had lost them. And, Reggie thought, he'd lost them to something he didn't understand. Wesley Blake had put his finger right on it.

You had to have the magic.

"You all fail to understand what will happen here!" Rick said. "Now, I'm all for Max, just like the next man. It was never my suggestion that Max step down entirely—just that he step aside for awhile!"

"No," Blake said flatly. "I say that we support our own." He leaned forward suddenly. "All right, now. We all know the situation. There are lesser stockholders who will be affected, of course, but we're the board, and the ball is in our hands. Let's lay it down on the table for a vote."

"I intend to abstain," Max said softly. "That way there can be no tie vote."

"Commendable, Max," Rick muttered. "All right. Let's get on with the vote. All in favor of Max stepping down—just for a few months—say aye and raise your hand!"

One hand went up—his own.

Niles wet his lips, started to raise his hand, then lowered it with a sharp slam on the table. "Hell, no! A man is innocent until he's proven guilty in this country!"

"Good for you, Niles!" Reggie approved enthusiastically.

"Maybe this should have been an anonymous vote," Max suggested.

"I don't think it needs to be anonymous," Wes said. "Everyone here is aware that you would not be offended by a vote against you, Max. Now, all in favor of leaving things as they are, say aye and raise your hand."

Four hands shot up and ayes filled the room thunderously.

Rick had lost, and he didn't look a bit pleased. He stood up almost immediately. "You know that I'm really all for you, Max. It's just the park that I'm worried about. You understand, don't you?"

"Oh, yes, of course, I understand," Max returned quietly.

Rick turned and started to stalk away from the table. As if on second thought, he bowed slightly to Reggie. "Now that I know you're over the past, Regina, I'll just keep trying until I do hit a free night with you," he said quietly.

Thank God, he didn't wait for an answer.

The moment he was out the door, Reggie wanted to leap up and shout.

She managed not to do so. Both Jesse and Niles were still looking somewhat worried. "Max," Jesse said, "we do have to watch the publicity on this like a bunch of hawks," he said solemnly.

"And we will!" Reggie assured him.

"I intend to. I thank you all for your votes of confidence in me," Max said. Then he stood abruptly. "If you'll excuse me, I'll let my secretary know that she needn't type up my resignation.''

Max left, followed by Jesse and then Niles, both pausing to say goodbye to Wes, and then to kiss Reggie on the cheek.

The moment they were gone, Reggie leaped up, having realized suddenly that she had been left all alone with her sandy-haired nemesis.

But even as she stood, a hand of iron came falling over her own.

"Where do you think you're going?" he asked lightly.

She couldn't have freed her hand if she had really tried, she knew. She felt a flush coming to her cheeks. "I—I have work to do, of course. It was nice to meet you, Mr. Blake. I appreciate your support of my brother. Even if you are somewhat of a shameless, arrogant snoop!" she added in a sudden rush.

He laughed softly. A dangerous laugh. She felt it inside and out.

"You're not going anywhere, Miss Delaney."

"I'm not?" she inquired, her ire rising.

He shook his head slowly. Those gold eyes seemed to slice right through her.

"You promised me dinner."

"Oh, but I didn't! That was just—"

"Oh, but you did."

"I can't possibly—"

"Oh, but you must!"

She did try to pull her hand away. He stood, never losing his grip, his eyes never faltering from hers.

She gritted her teeth. "I need to see Max—"

"Running to your brother?" he asked. "Do you need him to defend yourself from me?"

She inhaled sharply, then a dark winged brow rose high against her forehead. "Why? Do I need defending? Are you threatening me?"

"Not in any way," he replied politely. She didn't know how, but she was suddenly closer to him. Close enough to feel the pounding of the heart and the heat radiating from his taut, hard-muscled form. "But you did promise me dinner. And people do keep their promises to me."

"I—"

"I especially think that you should."

She lifted her chin. "And why is that?"

"Well, if your brother isn't guilty of some kind of foul play, then someone else is."

Reggie shrugged uncomfortably. She'd thought of that, but hadn't given it much consideration. She gasped suddenly. "And you think that I might be guilty!"

"I didn't say that."

"Well, you might as well have!" she exclaimed. She backed away from him, tugging at her wrist. "And what about you? I understand that you were at the wedding, that you knew Daphne—"

"Yes, that's right, I was there. I knew her." He smiled. "But I didn't know her like you knew her."

"We're talking in the past tense! We don't even know that anything has really happened. Daphne was rude and cruel and flighty. She might be on an island in the sun somewhere, just imagining what this is doing to poor Max."

"Ah! You didn't like her much, did you?"

Reggie gasped again—more at what she had given away so quickly than at the scope of his perception.

"Do you know that you are brash, arrogant and rude?" she accused him.

"Only when I need to be."

She stared at him, still tugging at her hand. She was amazed when he pulled her close once again. The warmth of his breath touched her face and seemed to start all kinds of fires in her again.

"But when it's necessary, Miss Delaney, I am anything I need to be. Right now, it's necessary. I'm going to find out the truth, Regina. I'm going to find out the whole truth, about everyone. Now, you can be in this with me, or you can be against me. But I swear to you, when I'm done, I will know everything. Everything. Now, are you coming with me, or not?"

Chapter 4

*T*he truth...

Reggie could hear Wes Blake's words ring in her ears—and feel the force of his fingers around her wrist—throughout the remainder of the day.

She had been convinced at first that he had meant to drag her away to dinner then and there—before they'd even had lunch!—but after making sure that she wasn't going anywhere, he had suddenly turned to leave the room.

"I'll meet you in front at seven," he had said. She'd been tempted to cry after him that she wouldn't be there, but he had spun around before she could do so. "Seven!" he'd repeated, as if daring her to make the statement she was longing to give.

She didn't have to say anything at all. She could just not show up!

"Was that seven you said?" she'd inquired sweetly.

She'd seen the quick tightening of his facial muscles, and she'd been glad that he didn't walk toward her then. For if he had, she might have taken a few cowardly steps back.

"Seven," he'd said once again. To her irritation, she'd remained still. As he turned to leave, she'd been startled to realize that he moved with a little limp. One that was almost imperceptible. But there.

"Damn him!" she'd said the moment he was out of the room.

Now she reminded herself that he had helped to save Max and her—and Dierdre's DinoLand. He wasn't helping because of her, she knew. He was helping because of Max. So he should have dinner with Max!

Stand the man up...could she do it? Should she do it?

Something in her said that he had come through when they needed someone to come through. Something else inside her said he was far too arrogant, and that he expected to have his every command obeyed. Yet something else told her that he was having an effect on her whether she liked it or not. He was making her feel things, think things. Things she hadn't thought about since...

There was work to be done. She didn't dare think about those things now. And maybe she wouldn't see Wes again. Maybe she would stand him up and she wouldn't have to wonder about the man and the effect he had on her.

Actually, she was never sure if she intended to show up for dinner or not. As it happened, she was called into a meeting with Niles, another of their character performers called in sick and a replacement couldn't be found, and in the end she had to help make sandwiches at Dierdre's Deli.

It was now eight-thirty, and the park—still on late spring hours even though temperatures made it seem like summer—had been closed for an hour and a half. The last of the gift shops was closing when she took off her shoes and walked barefoot over the cooling asphalt to her office. The night crew was sweeping up wrappers and cigarette butts and whatever hadn't been cleaned up during the day.

Even the cleanup crew was short of workers. She knew just how short when she came across her brother sweeping the broad expanse of entryway to the main cave. He looked up, frowning, as she appeared from the shadows of the cave.

"You're supposed to be at dinner," he said, pointing a finger at her. He was so accusing! As if she had failed to appear for royalty.

Or a financial backer, she thought wryly.

But Wes Blake was a friend Max cared about—that much had always been obvious. "Max! He's your friend—you should have gone to dinner."

"You agreed to dinner!"

"He was just helping me get out of dinner with Rick Player!"

"I don't think so, Reggie."

"All right—he means to give me the third degree. He means to dig into our lives."

Max was silent.

"Well?"

"Maybe."

Reggie sighed. "Well, at least he's on your side," she murmured.

"He believes in me," Max said. "But..."

"But what?"

"If he did find skeletons in the closet, he'd drag them out."

"Wonderful. I didn't mean to stand him up, but maybe I'm glad that I did!"

"Why did you? What are you still doing here?" he asked accusingly.

"What are *you* still doing here?" she demanded in turn.

She heard the grating of his teeth and knew that Max was annoyed with her. "Reggie—"

"Max."

"All right," he said softly. "I'd be here whether employee resignations were pouring in by the hour or not. It feels good to be out here. Good to be moving."

"Good to use the energy?" Reggie suggested. She curled her bare feet beneath her and sat down on the asphalt Max had just swept.

He smiled at her. Still in his suit, he seemed incongruous with the industrial-sized broom. But then again, she must have seemed incongruous in her red tailored suit, plopped upon the ground. He smiled suddenly, leaning on the broom handle. "We always promised each other that the park would be clean. Remember when we were afraid to hire too many employees? We always swept up then."

"I remember," she said softly. She wanted to stand up, to put her arms around him. But as close as they were, Reggie knew that he didn't want her sympathy right now.

"We're going to survive this, Max."

He started to sweep again. "Yeah. Well, the park deserves to survive."

"And so do we, Max!"

He stopped again. "God, Reggie, if this—this thing—winds up falling on you, too—"

"Oh, Max, don't! It's not going to fall on me. I won't let it. Maybe nothing will happen. Maybe Daphne will walk in on us tomorrow morning, laughing—"

"I wish she would. I really wish she would," Max said softly. He smiled ruefully. "But I don't think so."

Reggie didn't think so, either.

"Poor Daphne. But she really was such a bitch," Max reflected.

"You married her," Reggie reminded him.

"And though you always knew it was a mistake, you never said a word to me about her. I knew, though, of course. I always knew how you felt."

Reggie raised her hand limply. "Sorry." She was silent for a minute. "Why did you marry her?"

Max shrugged, dropping the broom and sitting down beside her. "I'll be damned if I know," he said at last. And then he smiled. A real smile. "Sex, maybe."

"Max!"

"You asked." He wagged a finger at her suddenly. "You haven't answered me. Why are you still here? You know, you did agree to go to dinner with Wes."

"I just got—busy," she said lightly.

"He's not going to be happy."

"Oh, Max, I don't mean to jeopardize—"

"You're not going to jeopardize anything as far as I'm concerned. You're usually so perceptive about people. Wes won't betray me—no matter how you behave toward him. He's not another Rick Player," Max said bitterly.

"Then—"

"Hey—this is between you and him, sweet cakes." Max laughed. "I'm just warning you—he's not going to be pleased."

She felt a shiver seize her and clamped down hard on her jaw, annoyed with herself. Why should she care what Wes Blake felt or thought? With any luck, he would just go away.

He wasn't going to go away. Somehow she knew it.

The adrenaline seemed to come rushing through her again. He did make her think. And shiver.

And feel.

"I take it women don't usually stand him up?" she said to Max, determined to break the silence before her brother could start to wonder what was really going on in her mind.

"*People* don't usually stand him up," Max said. "Men or women. I'm just warning you."

"Well, you might have warned me that he was about our own age!" she told her brother.

One of his dark brows shot up. "I didn't know that you assumed him to be anything other."

She flushed slightly. "Well, I did. I thought he was some eccentric old millionaire."

Max burst out with laughter. It was good to hear it.

"Why did you assume that? You knew we were in the service together."

"Yes, but I thought he was one of your officers. Older. You know, the career military type."

Max shrugged. "Well, he was that. Until our last war. Now he feels that there's just too much shrapnel in his leg."

"His left leg," Reggie murmured.

Max's eyes narrowed at her. "Yes," he said.

She lowered her lashes. He was watching her too intently. She professed, with a loud yawn, "Tomorrow is going to be another long day."

"They all get longer and longer don't they?"

"Max—"

"Sorry." He stood, reaching a hand down to her. "Come on. I'll take you home."

"I have my car."

"Leave it. I'll get you at eight. That should be early enough to start another round of torture."

"Max, we can't let it become torture."

"If we do," he murmured bitterly, "I really will have let her won!"

"We've got to hold the magic."

"You've always had the magic, Reggie. Always." He shrugged suddenly. "Come on. Let's get out of here for the night, eh?"

When they reached her house, Reggie was surprised that he saw her to the door. He took her key and opened the front door for her and looked around.

"What is it?" she asked him.

He shook his head. "Nothing. I'm just feeling cautious. Hey, do me a favor. Call Wes tomorrow and explain what happened, huh?"

She nodded. "Sure."

Gritting her teeth, she watched him leave. Damn Daphne. Even if she was dead. Oh, God, how awful!

she chastised herself. I didn't mean it, God, I didn't mean it.

But she felt hollow despite her protestations, and the questions plagued her while she showered and slipped into bed. She was afraid that she would stay awake all night thinking about her ex-sister-in-law.

But she didn't. She was exhausted. She fell asleep almost the minute that her head hit the pillow. And when she dreamed, it wasn't about Max. Or Daphne.

She dreamed about a dinosaur. An oddly trim, lean dinosaur. It was coming out of the shadows. Stalking her.

It became leaner. More dangerous. Hard. Sharp. Suddenly there was light. Warmth. She knew she should run, but she was attracted to the warmth.

Then she realized that it wasn't a dinosaur coming toward her at all. It was Wesley Blake. Slow, purposeful. He moved like a tiger in the night. Set on his prey. Sure of it. Determined in his pursuit.

She was his prey.

And still she didn't move. She waited. He came closer and closer. And she felt the gold fire of his eyes and the touch of his hand. . . .

She had promised Max that she would apologize to Wes.

Max had given him an office just down the hallway from her own, but when she stopped by, he wasn't in it. Damn him. She'd had her speech all ready. It wasn't going to be easy to apologize. She could have done it without stuttering or faltering, if she had just done it right away.

She swallowed her annoyance and the entire tug of emotions caused by the man and hurried to her own office. It was going to be another very busy day.

If Max was going to remain at the helm, they were going to have to be very careful. She stared at the phone on her desk for a moment.

Even her phone was a dinosaur. It was David Diplodocus. David's big, friendly body was the bulk of the phone, and his massive, curling tail was the mouthpiece and the receiver. She loved their creations, she really did. At the moment, though, she wished she had an ordinary phone.

She picked up David's tail and started dialing. She was going to call on every friend she had ever made in the media.

Luckily, there were a number of them.

She called Niles in his office and spoke to him about what they would and wouldn't say. Then she started with her round of people. There was a lot in her favor, she thought thankfully, when she reached Fran Rainier, entertainment editor of a major paper. Max Delaney hadn't exactly courted the press in the past, but no one seemed to be able to default him as a human being. She was glad she had called Fran. The silver-haired widow was a grandmother of five, a no-nonsense lady who didn't believe in sensationalism as a way to sell papers.

"Well, of course, we were wondering here what would happen," Fran told her. "As soon as we saw the headlines on that rag *Tongue Tattler*—"

"Um, well, we assumed that everyone would be wondering what had happened once it came out. I'm sure you've gotten a lot of the facts already. Her apartment was discovered in a complete upheaval, and her little yacht, *Daphne's Dare,* was found sunk out in the lake. The police believe that a hole was purposely bored out in the bottom, then filled with some kind of makeshift caulking that would dissolve with time in the water. But I assure you, there's been no arrest. There hasn't even been a warning of possible charges against Max. They've been divorced over a year, you know."

"Yes," Fran agreed, and she chuckled softly. "I'm a good friend, dear. You had best not sound quite so defensive with your next calls!"

Reggie sighed. "You're right. I'll try."

"It's going to get worse if they find a body," Fran warned Reggie.

"Much worse," Reggie agreed glumly. "But it's so unfair—"

"Yes, it is unfair. I know Max Delaney. He has his temper, and he has his ways. But if he was going to kill Daphne, the man would have throttled her right out in the open, years ago! Don't worry on my account. I'll write a stirring article about his wonderful character and make it sound as if anyone suspecting him of foul play must be downright un-American! Biased reporting, and if you repeat a word of what I've said—"

"Never! Never!" Reggie promised.

Soon she hung up the receiver. She had several more calls to make, and as she made them, she became more and more grateful that she had called Fran first. She was careful not to sound too defensive. She thought the calls all went well.

Then the interoffice line buzzed and she picked it up. "Yes?"

"Reggie. It's Max."

"Max, it's going super. I just spoke with—"

"Reggie, trust me, it's not going so super. Ten more resignations in the last hour. Can you get to Dino-Shoe Falls right away? We're missing a dance hall girl for the afternoon show."

She swore silently. She couldn't even remember the numbers for the dance hall review.

"Which character?" She asked.

"Patricia."

"I'm on my way."

The one good thing, Reggie decided as she hurried to the dinner theater stage and into a dressing room, was that Max didn't give her much time to worry about what she would be doing. She was alone in the dressing room, although there should have been an assistant there. She found Patricia's bright red dance outfit and the garish black net hose that went with it. She tried to remember all the songs and words. It was a forty-five-minute show, most of it ad-lib, and a whole lot of it audience participation. She'd be all right.

Out in the wings of the dinner theater stage she found the rest of the cast—Bob Winwood, Stevie Gentry and Alise Guest. The three were young, in their midtwenties, and had all started here together after graduating from a fine arts college. Max had given them their first big break. He paid them well.

"That Lorna had no right to walk out—especially on such short notice!" Alise assured Reggie with a quick hand squeeze. "Don't you worry, we're not going anywhere."

"And we'll make up for any mistakes you make!" Bob promised her cheerfully.

"Thanks," Reggie murmured dryly. Well, hell, she probably would make mistakes!

They were being announced, so there was no more time to talk. Within seconds she and Alise were running out on stage, fluffing their boas into the faces of their audience and bursting into song and dance. Soon Bob came along on his bucking stuffed bronco-saur, the bad guy, ready to shoot up the saloon. Then Stevie, the blond, blue-eyed hero, showed up, ready to save the day.

Patricia's character was the flirt, the slightly dangerous lady, who fell in love with the bad guy. It was her job to race through the audience and convince them all that Bob's character mustn't be hanged by the masses. She had a great song, one that used the whole audience. It was fun. It was so much fun that—for a matter of minutes—she was able to forget just how serious their problems were.

She strutted through the audience. She looped her boa around a bald man's neck and asked his wife if she could borrow him for just a minute. His pink-cheeked, good-humored wife said that Reggie could borrow him for as long as she liked. Reggie assured her that she didn't take any man for longer than a few minutes and turned her attention to the fellow behind him, one who had been sitting in the shadows. She stretched out a black-net-clad leg to climb up on his lap, flipping her boa out again.

And then she nearly screamed.

It was him again. Blake. Wesley Blake.

Now he was in casual light beige chinos and a maroon knit shirt. He had almost blended in with the saloon decor.

Damn. Over a hundred men out here, and she had found his lap to sit on.

She fought the panic rising in her when his gaze locked onto hers. He was smiling. He had to be angry with her. *People didn't stand him up.* But she had.

Max had suggested that she apologize, and she'd tried, but he didn't know that. And the way he was staring at her...

She needed to escape, but she was in the middle of a show!

"What did you find out there, Patricia?" Alise called out to her.

Damn. She'd been silent. Dead silent. In the middle of a show. With an entire audience watching her. Waiting.

But, oh... she hadn't been expecting this!

She could feel the growing warmth of his lap beneath her. His arms had fallen lightly around her, and though she knew that he would release her instantly the moment she got up to go, she could feel the strength of them, too, and it was oddly disturbing. She was breathing his after-shave, something very light and subtle, something that combined with a natural scent and made her acutely aware that he was the opposite sex. She could almost feel his freshly shaven cheeks against her own.

And most of all, she was aware of his eyes. She could feel them, too. Glittering gold, with amusement, with more. They stared into her own. She grew hotter. His lips were curling into a smile. A knowing smile. As if she had come here on purpose. The smile was wicked, wicked.

The heat inside her seemed to flash and grow, streaking throughout her body. She wanted to jump up immediately, to forget the role that she played, to run in swift, sure panic.

Maybe he knew that he had that effect on her.

Okay, maybe Max had been right for a long time. Maybe she did need to get a life. But Wesley Blake seemed to be just a little too confident for her liking. Perhaps she had been out of the mainstream for a long time. She still wasn't going to give an inch to this stranger.

Her eyes narrowed. She flipped the boa around his neck and pulled tight.

"Oh, I did find a live one out here, I did, I did!" she drawled to Alise.

There was a slight shifting in Wes's legs. "Very much alive," he murmured huskily.

The folks closest to them heard him. They started laughing.

Bob was a definite showman. He was down from the stage immediately, twirling his fake black mustache with his fingers.

"Patricia, honey, I'm over here. Remember me?"

She leaned forward, slipping her arms around Wes's neck, letting her eyes focus hugely on his. "What was that?"

The audience howled.

It was a mistake. She felt his body tensing beneath hers. Felt the warmth increase.

Felt his eyes. Warm. Acute. And she saw the slow curve of his smile and felt a steady sinking in her heart.

"I said, I'm over here, honey!" Bob repeated. More laughter. He sighed dramatically and took a huge step over to the two of them. "Excuse me, sir, would you?" He set a finger underneath Reggie's chin, turning her face to his. "Patricia, remember me?" He fell down on a knee before her. "Why, I'm going to cast aside my evil ways and make an honest woman out of you, honey! You're in love with me, honey—'scuse me, sir, your lap is in the way there! You've made an honest man of me, Patricia."

"Oh, yes!" She exclaimed, blinking. "And your name was what...?"

Again, the audience filled with laughter. It was probably one of the best shows they had ever done. It was killing her.

"Martin. Martin Van der Crime. Ah, excuse me, sir, she does have to marry me, sir."

"I do?"

"She does?"

"Yep. You can't have her, sir!"

"I can't?" Wes said. Another smile flickered across his features. "Why not?"

"'Cause I'm in this show, sir, and you're not!" Bob told him.

She liked the way Wes laughed then. Good-naturedly. Willing to be part of the fun. Willing to believe in the magic.

Just as he had been that morning. With Dierdre Dinosaur.

"Well, heck, if you put it that way..." Wes murmured regretfully.

She jumped off his lap. She didn't want to fall for this much fantasy herself. She knew the other side to the man. There was a hard core to him as rigid as steel. He was interested in her. Ah, yes. He was interested.

Because he had come for the truth. And he seemed to see her as a way to get to that truth.

They were still in the middle of a show. Bob was staring at her, waiting.

He had cast a cue line right into her lap.

"Martin, oh, yes, Martin! I'll be delighted if you'll make an honest woman out of me. Marriage! Why, yes, marriage! It sounds just wonderful."

"And you'll pledge your heart to me forever?" Bob said dramatically, his hands atop each other and playfully palpitating over his heart.

"Why, sure, honey!" she said. Bob slipped an arm around her and they started through the audience toward the stage.

But she was a showman herself. She couldn't help flicking the boa over her shoulder. It flounced over Wesley's shoulder and trailed across his face. Once again, the audience howled.

She and Bob leaped on the stage with Alise and Stevie and they all joined in for the final number about the triumph of good over evil. There was wonderful applause, and the foursome hurried off the stage.

"Oh, that was great, great!" Alise laughed as soon as they had reached the wings. "Gosh, Reggie, it would be wonderful if you would work with us every day. That was one of the best shows we've ever done."

"It was great," Bob agreed, pulling off his fake mustache. "The audiences here are usually fun, but it's rare to find a total stranger that you can play off of so easily! That guy was wonderful—"

"Thanks," a husky voice interrupted. "But I'm not a total stranger."

Reggie stiffened immediately. There he was again. Wesley Blake. Lounging negligently against the wall of the short hallway leading to the dressing rooms. His hands were in his pockets. He seemed so casual, so easy.

All but those eyes of his . . .

"Oh, so he's a friend of yours!" Bob said, grinning. He offered a hand to Wes. "Hi! Any friend of Reggie's is welcome. And to you, especially— thanks!"

Reggie forced a smile to her lips. "He's not exactly a friend of mine," she murmured. "This is Wesley Blake. Major stockholder in our corporation."

"And don't you forget it!" he said lightly. Reggie introduced the three performers. Wes shook Bob's hand, Stevie's, then Alise's. She had a puppy-dog look about her brown eyes that made Reggie long to slap some sense into her.

"You're wonderful!" Alise said. "I mean—you were wonderful. The audience was just eating it all up."

He smiled at her. "But all to no avail."

"What?" Alise said. She still had his hand.

His grin deepened. "Bob was right."

"How so?"

"Well, he was the one in the show. He walked away with the girl."

"Oh!" Alise laughed.

"But I do have a dinner date with her, right?" he said, looking at Reggie.

"Do you?" Reggie murmured.

"Don't I?" He looked at Alise. "I was supposed to have a dinner date with her last night. Somehow, she eluded me."

"That's terrible!" Alise told him.

"That's what I thought."

To her annoyance, Reggie felt hot color flash to her cheeks. "I'm afraid I was busy making dinner for others," she murmured. "I am sorry—"

"Really?" he asked politely.

She could hear her own teeth grinding. "I tried to reach you this morning—"

"Did you?"

"Yes, I did."

She didn't owe him anything! Still she felt the most curious edge as she watched him. Was he really angry with her? She couldn't tell.

"Well," he murmured, "we do have a dinner date tonight, right?"

"So it seems," Reggie agreed less than graciously, her eyes suddenly downcast. Was he a wolf in sheep's clothing? No, just a wolf. The man made no pretenses.

And the thing that made her so uneasy was herself. He was attractive. Too attractive. And she was just a means to an end for him, while he intended to pry into every single aspect of her brother's life. And maybe even into her own.

Again, she felt defensive. Every barrier had to be kept in place against this man!

"Well," Alise said with a soft sigh, "you two have a nice dinner. I guess it will be pizza and beer for me with this duo!"

"Gee, Bob, doesn't she make that sound like a great compliment?" Stevie asked.

"Boy, that's right. I could get a Mel Gibson complex, just listening to her!"

Alise gave him a swat in the arm. "See ya!" she said to Reggie, leading the other two down the hallway toward the dressing rooms.

Reggie suddenly felt tense and vulnerable. She pointed in their direction. "I'll just change—"

He shook his head. "I don't think so."

"What do you mean, you don't think so!" Reggie demanded. "I'm dressed as a nineteenth-century floozy—"

"Hey, that's your problem. I'm not leaving you for a minute. Not tonight."

"Oh, now you are being absurd!" Reggie said. She started to turn. He caught hold of her arm.

And the hold was fierce. Unyielding.

He drew her around to face him. She saw that his jaw was twisted and set. He was a man determined.

One who didn't seem to give any quarter.

"Let me go!" she insisted in a whisper.

"Not on your life."

"I have to change!"

"Feel free. But from this minute on, Miss Delaney, whither thou goest, I goest also."

Reggie tried to jerk free. "How dare you!"

"Trust me. I dare anything. I don't appreciate being stood up."

"I didn't mean—"

"I'm sure you didn't. I could tell yesterday afternoon just how anxious you were to have dinner with me."

"I'm going to go change—"

"That's fine. I won't mind at all."

Reggie stared at him, ready to scream.

But she sensed suddenly that screaming wouldn't get her anywhere at all.

"I'm not leaving your side," he reminded her softly, gold eyes glittering in challenge. "So tell me, Miss Delaney, just what shall it be?"

Chapter 5

He had to hand it to her, Wes thought an hour later.

Miss Regina Delaney could be a very stubborn woman.

They were seated at a table in Larkin's Lobster House, a well-known fish house with an excellent reputation and a crowded dining room, and his companion for the evening—he didn't dare call her a date!—was still clad in a garish red old-western-saloon-floozy's outfit, complete down to the outrageous fishnet stockings.

She wasn't happy about her mode of dress. She had come through the entryway as quickly as possible, stoically ignored the stares of the hostess and maître d' and hurried to the booth in the back.

The place boasted a fantastic salad bar, but Miss Delaney had opted to turn it down, choosing a small spinach salad with her twin lobsters. She wasn't about to get up.

He would have felt guilty about her discomfort, except for the fact that she *could* have changed. All she had to do was bring him along with her right to the door of the dressing room. Maybe she hadn't realized that he would stop there. Maybe she was just a little bit afraid of him.

And maybe that was good.

And maybe it was a good thing that she seemed so determined to keep a certain distance from him. After the dinosaur play in the park that first day, things had gone rather badly. She seemed to think that he was out to hurt her and Max in some way. He wasn't. He'd do anything in the world for either of them and he was just as convinced as Reggie that Max was innocent. She didn't understand. And he wanted her to. Too much. His attraction to her was frightening. Maybe because he'd never felt quite this kind of thing before.

This type of thing... He growled inwardly. He wanted her. It was simple. It wasn't anything magical.

It was just strong. Harder, stronger, more insistent than any feeling he'd had before. Max's twin was beautiful. But he didn't think it was the beauty. He'd known many beautiful women. Shelley had been beautiful, and even with her, the longing had been something that had grown.

Longing and love. He had loved Shelley, he thought almost numbly. He scarcely knew Reggie Delaney.

But still, there were things that created the longing in him that were far stronger than any simple draw of beauty. She was a contrast of so many things. There was a shyness about her—unless she was cloaked in dinosaur foam or in the flagrant crimson of the dance hall girl. There was something in her eyes that spoke of innocence.

Yet when it came to defending her brother, she was a lioness.

And then again, there had been the way she had been with him. When she had been dressed as Dierdre Dinosaur, she'd been having fun—a lot of it. She didn't mind teasing, and she didn't mind playing. But she did like the cloak of anonymity.

He sighed softly, watching her sip an iced tea and look around the room from beneath the rich shade of her luxurious dark lashes. She was obviously wishing she had sent her pride to the wind and had gone ahead and changed into street clothing—with or without him.

He suddenly wished they could start over again.

But they couldn't. You could never go back in life. He knew that. Maybe he could convince her that he wasn't her enemy.

But then again, maybe he was her enemy in a way, because he would use her to get at the truth if he had to, and he did have to get at the truth.

He couldn't help teasing her, just a bit. He leaned forward. "Others may not appreciate it to the fullest extent, but have I told you yet? That's really a great dress."

She smiled sweetly, setting her tea glass on the table. "Have I told you yet, Mr. Blake? I really think that you should eat dirt!"

He laughed. "Maybe I had that coming."

"You certainly did."

Their waitress arrived with their lobsters. They looked great. Cracked, broiled with butter—just flown in from Maine that morning, according to the placards on the walls.

"Would you like another beer with your meal, sir?" the waitress asked him. He glanced at his bottle. "Sure. One more. Reggie? How about a glass of wine?"

"I don't care for wine, thank you."

"A beer then."

"I don't—"

"Just a beer for me then, please," he told the waitress pleasantly. "Sorry—my date here is just a wondrous pillar of virtue."

He thought Reggie's smile was about to crack, but she kept it in place for the waitress, who had been looking wide-eyed at Reggie's costume.

"One must try to be virtuous when out with the date from hell!" she said with a soft, sweet sigh.

The waitress looked at them both as if they were crazy, but kept up a valiant smile, then hurried away for another beer.

"You're just staring at your food," Wes commented.

"I'm waiting for you."

He passed her a shell cracker. "I'm all set."

She cracked into her first claw. She did it so hard that a piece of shell flew straight into the air, then landed on Wes's plate with a big clicking sound. He stared at her, arching a brow. She flushed slightly. "Sorry."

"Are you sure you wouldn't like a beer or something? Anything, just to relax? Or are you really such a pillar of virtue?"

"Well, you know, really, I don't believe in sloshing my way through a date—"

"Aha! So it is a date!" he said with a laugh. "Well, trust me, I appreciate the fact that you don't want to slosh your way through it. I don't want to slosh through it, either. But truly, I don't think that one drink would send you passing out limply in my arms." She gazed at his arms as he said the words. He could have sworn that a little shudder passed through her. Was it really all that bad?

"I will try to keep my food on my plate," she promised.

He shrugged. "Hey. There's not much you can do to bother me." He leaned forward and whispered softly, "I mean, after all, I'm out with you already. And look at the way you're dressed."

Her cracker went slicing through shell again. This time the entire claw went flying up. It landed in his water glass.

"I wasn't drinking it anyway," he assured her quickly.

"I wasn't apologizing," she said.

"The waitress is coming. Sure you don't want anything?"

"Yes. I want to be eating with that elderly gentleman over in the corner there. Or with that couple with the toddler spitting applesauce over his bottle."

"I meant, do you want anything to drink?"

"No!"

The waitress brought his beer. Reggie turned to her. "I'll take whatever you have on draft."

"Can I, er, help you with that lobster?" Wes asked Reggie politely.

"No!"

The waitress brought Reggie's beer quickly, set it down and departed even more quickly. Reggie instantly picked up and swallowed down a long draft, eyeing him with a great deal of hostility over the rim of the glass.

She set the glass down with a little smack against the table. "There. Is that an improvement?"

"Hey," he murmured lightly, lifting his hands palms upward, "anything is an improvement."

She picked up her lobster cracker with a vengeance. Her eyes were flashing a beautiful emerald color.

Dinner could get very dangerous, he warned himself.

"You insisted on dinner," she reminded him. She had managed to get the tail section of her lobster split. She set into the white meat with the little three-pronged fork she had been given. She speared a morsel of meat and set it delicately in her mouth.

He found himself staring at her mouth. She went for another bite, finding the meat, dipping it into the melted butter, placing it in her mouth.

A little sheen remained on her lips from the drawn butter. He found himself still staring at her in fascination. Growing warm. She had a beautiful mouth.

Just as he had earlier, he mused that it was really the kind of mouth that almost asked to be kissed. Beautifully defined. Full. Sensual. Glistening now, and so enticing that he almost reached out a finger to touch her lips.

"You did, remember?"

"What?"

"You insisted on this dinner. If you're not pleased—"

He forced his eyes from her mouth and focused on his beer glass. He drew his fingers idly around the rim. "Oh, I'm pleased. Just as pleased as punch."

She stopped chewing. She leaned forward. A stray tendril of ebony hair had escaped from the saloon girl's knot at her nape and danced softly against the ivory beauty of her face. She spoke softly, huskily. "All right. I'm supposed to be grateful for what you did for Max, I suppose. I am grateful. But you're supposed to be Max's friend. You're supposed to support him. You did, it's done. We're all grateful."

He sighed and leaned closer to her. "Reggie, I do have faith in Max. That's the point here. If Max isn't guilty of an evil deed, then it seems that someone else is."

"What do you mean, *if?*" she asked, blinking. Ink-dark lashes fell over the beautiful green of her eyes, then rose again. "We know that Max—"

"We both agree that Max is innocent," he said. "But since we agree that Max is innocent, then we have to assume that someone else is guilty."

"But—" She faltered for just a second. "But we're not even sure that anything has happened to Daphne—"

"Oh, come off it! Or save it for the press," he said.

Her cracker was in her fingers again, and her fingers were very tense. Oh, no. Lobster shell was flying again, and this time it wasn't coming his way.

A piece of Reggie's claw went flying up, up.

It landed with a soft thud right in front of the little toddler who was busy decorating his Sesame Street bottle with his applesauce.

The child looked up instantly, a huge smile spreading across his cheeks.

His parents were not so amused. Startled, they both stared toward him and Reggie.

"I'm so sorry—" Reggie began.

"You can dress her up," Wes said with an exaggerated sigh, "but you still can't take her anywhere! Ouch!"

She had kicked him beneath the table.

It didn't matter, but the toddler's parents were laughing. "Hey, it's a perfect ending to a perfect meal," the young father said wryly. The couple were standing, extracting their son from his high chair. "Hey, you're Regina Delaney, aren't you?" the man asked.

Reggie nodded slowly. Wes was startled at the emotion that swept through him as he saw the wariness in her eyes. She was instantly afraid and defensive.

"Is this a publicity thing?" his wife asked, indicating her costume.

"No, it's, er—"

"It was a late night," Wes supplied.

She should have been grateful. She kicked him beneath the table anyway. "I can answer for myself!" she reproached him softly. She glared at him, then smiled at the couple. "It was a late night," she said pleasantly.

"Poor thing, you do look tired!" the woman said.

Reggie was tensing again, aware of the couple's obvious curiosity.

"Oh, no. I think it's her age. She's just haggard-looking all the time now," Wes said, sitting back.

She glared at him. With a look that could kill.

"Thirty," she said lightly. "You do have to watch out for it. It's downhill all the way after."

"And she should know. She's thirty-three," Wes supplied.

The couple laughed. "I don't think you look haggard at all!" the woman said.

Neither did Wes.

The woman continued. "Why, every time we've seen your picture in the news, my Joe here has commented on what a beautiful woman you are. And your brother, of course, is divine. And—" she hesitated a second, flashing a quick look at her husband "—and you should know that all the local people here are a hundred percent behind you and your brother. The park is wonderful. We love to go there. Our boy—" she glanced down to the baby in her arms "—our boy just loves the little people rides, and he's crazy about Dierdre and Dolly and David and the rest. And long before this, we've seen all the good that your brother tries to do, and we'll just never believe evil of him, we won't—"

"Martha!" the man said.

"Well, it's true!"

Reggie's lashes were over her cheeks. Then she looked up. "Thank you!" she said quietly. "Really, thank you. That means so much."

"Martha, let's leave them to eat in peace now," her husband said.

Wes laughed. "Don't worry about leaving us in peace. We're the ones who pelted you with the lobster shells, remember?"

The couple laughed. Reggie narrowed her eyes. They all said good-night to one another.

"You really do have to try to control your temper while dealing with lobster claws."

"Why?" she murmured, her eyes widening as she stared at him. "When I have such a stalwart and charismatic man to come so chivalrously to my defense?"

He laughed. "The most stalwart of defenders has to admit to the truth. You did pelt them with lobster shells."

"Shell. One lobster shell."

"Yes, but we're worried about headlines here, right? Can you imagine this one? R. Delaney Grows Violent In Lobster House. Eighteen-Month-Old Baby Attacked By Crimson Claw!"

"I didn't attack a baby."

"You were aiming at me?"

"I wasn't aiming at anyone!" She suddenly clenched her hands together in her lap. "Oh, can't you please just go home?"

He shook his head, suddenly serious. "Reggie, you know I can't."

"But—"

"This isn't just going to go away."

"The police are on it."

"Yes, and the police are on dozens of other crimes, too. I can't just let the board go on accepting Max's position. He has to be proved innocent. Not because of the law. But because of people. And this is a point that goes full circle. If Max is innocent, someone else is guilty. Reggie, has it ever occurred to you that you—and Max—could be in danger?"

"No," she said flatly. "Daphne was a wretched bitch. It was amazing that she and Max ever married in the first place."

"So tell me what you know."

She frowned, her eyes widening. He clenched his teeth suddenly, wishing he wouldn't react to her on such a gut level. Every once in a while he would just be looking at her, and in his mind's eye, she'd be half naked again. Then all naked . . .

But it wouldn't be just the flesh that would get him. It would be the sound of her voice, the emerald sizzle of her eyes. Whatever, he really couldn't explain it. There'd just be fire, shooting through him.

"About Daphne?"

"About Daphne. Max. Everything."

She shook her head slightly, then took a reflective sip of her beer.

Foam clung to her lips for a moment. She caught it with the tip of her tongue.

Part of his stomach seemed to fall to his feet, and every limb and protrusion of his body went tense.

"Well," she murmured dryly, "Max even knew that she was a witch. He said that he married her for the sex."

"I can see that," Wes grunted. "Go on."

"They were just ill-suited. Max is very big on his charities. Daphne wouldn't have loaned her own mother a dime. She didn't care for the puppets—but she did love the prestige." She stared at him suddenly, pointedly. "But then, you should know this better than I. You went to their wedding. I didn't. He married her on such quick, wild impulse, I wasn't able to attend."

"Tell me about her disappearance."

"I'm sure you've seen the police reports—"

"I want to hear it from you."

She sighed, setting her wrists on the table. "All right. Cut and dried. As fast and as completely as I can. I didn't discover her gone—neither did Max. I barely saw her in the past year. Admittedly, Max did upon occasion. At the divorce, he had given her a nice settlement. He just wanted out. But they had been married. If she was in trouble, Max came. And she called. I don't think she had ever really believed Max would divorce her. Family and commitment mean so much to him."

"What one never has..." Wes murmured.

"Exactly," Reggie said coolly. "If her pipes were leaking, Max went over. Or he sent someone over. But on the day she was discovered missing, neither Max nor I was ever near her. She'd had a meeting with a reporter from that wretched *Tattler* paper. She was going out in her yacht on the lake in the morning. She was to meet him at one. At two o'clock, the reporter was sitting in front of her apartment door, still twirling his thumbs. Finally, he called the police. They called Max. Max didn't know anything. Ozzie Daniels—the reporter—managed to get them to call the manager and enter Daphne's apartment. It was found in total disarray. And of course, no sign of Daphne.''

"And the little yacht?"

"*Daphne's Dare*. It was found later the same day, sunk in the lake. The experts say a tiny hole had been bored, then filled with a resin. The boat didn't begin to sink until she was way out in the deep when the purposely poor caulking began to dissolve in the water.''

"And that's it. That's all they have," Wes mused. He knew the story. He'd gone to the police station before he'd come near Max, the park or Reggie.

He had just wanted to hear it from her. And he had wanted to hear the nuances in her voice. There were so many things he could learn from Reggie that he'd never learn from a black-and-white typed police report.

"They found prints," he said.

"Yes. In her apartment. Daphne's, mine—I had been there a few times."

"And Max's."

"Yes, and Max's. And Ozzie's and Rick Player's and even Jesse's. She had a party once, and had someone con them all into coming. The prints were all there."

"You really hated her, didn't you?" he asked.

He hadn't even seen her pick up the lobster cracker again. It crunched loudly.

A shell flew across the table. A mangled claw landed in his plate.

He looked at her.

"Can't finish it all, huh?"

"Are you accusing me of something?"

He smiled slowly. Her eyes were flashing. More dark hair was tumbling down. He was growing distracted. And damnably hot tremors were racing through his bloodstream. . . .

For a brief moment he closed his eyes. God, he should feel good. Really good. If he could just forget the rest, and let the feelings wash over him! It had been so long since he had experienced anything like this.

Even if it meant pain to come. Even the pain would be good. So much better than the numbness, the coldness, the emptiness that had haunted him for so long now.

"Are you?" she demanded.

"Reggie, you've got to look at everyone. Don't you see, to clear Max, you find the real perpetrator of the crime."

"There may not have been a crime—"

"You mean that Daphne may have trashed her own apartment and sunk *Daphne's Dare* herself."

"Exactly."

"It's possible."

"Possible, but—"

"Give me a list. Give me a lineup of people who knew and loved her."

"Hated her."

"Fine."

Reggie stared at him balefully then set her cracker and lobster down. Her wrists rested tensely on the table.

"All right, let's see. There was Rick Player. He was always hanging around Daphne. He loved to be at the same spot with her any time Max might be around. He liked to torture Max.''

''Did Max care? Was he bothered by Player's attention to her?''

Reggie shrugged. ''I don't think so. He seemed free from her once the divorce was over. But it was hard to tell.''

''So go on.''

''Um . . . ah, then there was Ozzie Daniels.''

''The sensationalist reporter?''

Reggie nodded. ''He could have been a good reporter, I think. A really good one. Except that he was given much more money for working on a scandal sheet and given a free rein to do what he pleased. Daphne was a weak link to him. She'd always give him some kind of a story.''

''What kind of a story did she intend to give him the day she disappeared?''

Reggie shook her head. ''I don't know,'' she said.

''Sounds like this Ozzie Daniels needed her around. She was good for him. And it sounds like Rick Player liked her, too.''

''Meaning?''

He shrugged. ''Who really hated her? Who stood to gain by her disappearance?''

Reggie sighed. ''I don't know!''

He leaned close to her. ''You have to know! There has to be someone.''

She lifted her hands. ''There's Niles, there's Jesse! Both of them despised the way she treated people.''

''And then . . .'' he murmured.

''Then what?''

''There's you,'' he said softly.

"What?" she exclaimed furiously.

"Max's twin, determined to defend him against a black-widow woman."

"Oh, you are despicable!" She gasped, leaning close to him.

God, he liked the way her eyes flashed. He liked the tick of her pulse against her throat.

"Then there's you!" she returned. "Max's financial backer, a man who met Daphne at their wedding! A man who stood to lose and lose big if Max was dragged through the mud! An ex-military man, a man with the strength and purpose and coldness of heart to do anything to protect his own interests!"

Her words sank over him like a sizzling blanket. This was not the way to make friends, he realized. But he wasn't supposed to be making friends. He was supposed to be discovering the truth. But every moment couldn't be a revelation.

And the one discovery he was making was that he was fascinated by his partner's sister.

"Coldness of heart?" he queried, as if deeply injured.

She threw her napkin on the table. "If you find this entire thing amusing—" Reggie broke off midsentence.

She'd been so angry. So damned angry. He had an answer for everything. He'd sat there through the entire meal, amused, intense, watching her every awkward movement, pouncing upon her mistakes.

It was his fault that a lobster shell had flown so damn far so damn many times!

His smile had been quick and his easy charm had disarmed the couple who had spoken to them. But he was not easy or charming or amused now. His eyes glittered like cold metal as they fell upon her.

And his fingers, around her wrist, were a vise that she couldn't fight.

"It isn't amusing. None of it is amusing," he assured her.

"Then—"

"Come on," he said. He released her wrist and stood, signaling to the waitress for their check. He tossed a number of bills on the table, thanked the waitress and reached for Reggie's hand again. "I'll take you home."

"I can get home by myself."

"Don't be absurd. If you called a cab, the driver would take you to the red-light district or the loony bin."

"I'll take my chances."

"Not on your life. I brought you out—I'll bring you home."

"I don't need a protector—"

"But maybe you do."

"I can manage on my own—"

"I'm sure that you can. But I won't let you."

His fingers tightened around her wrist. They didn't hurt her. They were just firm. As firm as steel.

She stared at him, then lifted her chin stubbornly. "You, Mr. Blake, are a pain in the backside. And if you don't let go of me this instant, I just might be tempted to scream."

"Oh?"

He still hadn't hurt her. But suddenly she was standing—close to him. The scent of him seemed to be filling her, and flashes of heat seemed to be dancing up and down her spine. She could nearly feel the rough-hewn texture of his cheek. His voice touched and caressed her.

"You're going to scream?" he murmured. A slow smile was curling into his lips. "You're the one dressed in red with fishnet stockings. Hmm. I should scream. Maybe you've been propositioning me. The outfit would impress the cops, I'm sure."

"You're out of your mind!" she whispered.

"Maybe. But I'm taking you home. Whether you scream or not. I'll walk you out—or carry you out. But I will see you home."

"You are a truly arrogant bastard!" she said angrily.

"Yeah. Maybe," he agreed.

His fingers curled around hers, and he led her out of the restaurant.

And before she knew it, she had given him her address, and he was taking her home. And even as his car sped along the highway, she felt the growing tremor of her heart. And the heat that steamed and smoldered in her system.

She would never let him stay, and yet she was certain he would try. But the really frightening part was...

It was exactly what she really wanted him to do.

Chapter 6

Reggie's house was somewhat away from the city and located in the surrounding farm, cattle and horse country that filled so much of the central part of the state. Her place wasn't exactly a farm, but it was an old Colonial set back on about three acres of land. There had been a house on the foundation as early as the 1840s when some of the first plantations had found their way down south, but that first house had burned to the ground in an Indian raid.

Around the turn of the century some gentleman farmer had built a Colonial on the site. Reggie had fallen in love with the house the second she had seen it and—armed with some of the first real money she and Max had ever made—she had bought the place within forty-eight hours. Even Caleb had loved it from the start.

Except that he had never been able to move into the house with her. The accident had occurred hours after she had signed the papers.

She didn't want to think about that tonight. The accident had been so long ago. But when she came upon the house in the dark like this—just as she and Caleb had come upon it that first time—she often couldn't help but think of him.

It was true that the pain was fading. No pain could last so intensely so long.

But the hurt was still there. The emptiness and the hurt. The kind of feeling that made it all the worse to think that there might be nothing left in this world for her except for men like Rick Player.

Well, she wasn't with Rick Player tonight. And suddenly she was trying to think about Caleb.

She couldn't quite do it. She couldn't quite summon his face to superimpose over that of the man beside her.

"You can let me off at the foot of the drive," she began, but quickly fell silent. He had taken her out; he was going to see her home.

His car pulled up the long bricked drive and came to rest in front of the house. She had timers for the lights, and Mrs. Martin had been in today anyway, so everything would be alight and welcoming.

He opened the driver's door of his handsome, dark green Jaguar and came around to her side. He opened the door and politely reached out a hand to help her from the car. She hesitated briefly then took it.

It wasn't that she was trying to be petty at the moment. It was just that contact with him caused so many emotions and sensations to come cascading down on her.

She wasn't ready for them. She hadn't felt the slightest tug of attraction in so long, and now...

Her cheeks started to burn. She stepped from the car and hurried past him, fumbling in her bag for her key. "I'm really quite all right now—"

He took the key from her fingers. "I can see that you're just fine," he told her dryly. He fit the key into the lock and pushed open the front door.

She thought she heard a sound—muffled and soft like a door closing in the house.

It was a sound that sent a river of chills sweeping along her spine. She was startled by the encompassing fear that suddenly seemed to blanket her.

Had the noise been real? It had been so damn soft. But as she looked into Wes's eyes in the bright light of the porch lantern, she knew instantly from his expression that she hadn't imagined the sound at all.

"Is someone else supposed to be here?" he asked.

She shook her head. "Unless Mrs. Martin stayed late. Except her car would be out here. What—"

"There's a back door?" he asked quickly.

"Yes—"

"Then that's what!" he exclaimed harshly. He pushed past her and followed the center hall to the back and to the left, past the huge old-fashioned kitchen and family room to the door that led to the backyard and the open pool.

Reggie ran along behind him. "Wait!" But he seemed to know where he was going. She ran after him, only vaguely aware that things seemed to be out of place. There wasn't anything massively askew. Her home hadn't been ravaged the same way Daphne's had been; things were just slightly out of kilter. The bottom drawer of the big mirrored bureau in the entryway was open just a hair. But she knew it had been closed that morning. And the seascape farther down the wall was tilted, as if someone had brushed it with a shoulder as he or she had rushed by it.

"Wait!" Reggie called again, but Wes was already in her kitchen, at the back door.

He had pushed it open. It hadn't been locked. He stood in the doorway looking at her. "Close this behind me. Lock it. Don't open it unless you hear my voice. My voice! No one else's. Understand!"

"Yes, but—"

"Lock the damn door behind me!"

He was gone, and the door slammed sharply in his wake. She stared at it for a moment. A moment too long.

"Lock it! Quickly."

She did so, then leaned against it, waiting, scarcely able to breathe.

Then, just seconds later, she heard the sharp explosion of a gunshot.

No, it could be a car backfiring....

But she didn't think so. Her neighbors were too far away. She hadn't seen anyone parked along the road.

Someone was shooting. At Wesley Blake.

She turned and threw open the door. "Wes!" she cried out. She heard another explosion and a whizzing sound. Close. Very close. Then she spun around, a scream escaping from her lips. The wood paneling on the wall behind her exploded with a soft thud as a bullet was embedded in it.

Then she was suddenly flying and lying flat on the ground with a tremendous weight and strength over her. She started to scream, but the weight was quickly up, and she fell silent as she stared into a pair of furious gold eyes.

"I told you to lock the door! You almost got yourself killed!"

"I'm sorry! Forgive me for trying to make sure that you didn't get *yourself* killed!"

He straddled her. The door was closed behind them. He must have slammed it shut when he came flying in to bring her to the ground.

It occurred to her, even as she met the fever of his gaze, that she very nearly had been killed. A bullet had flown by, just inches from her head. She swallowed hard, fighting the trembling that had begun inside her. And then, even as she felt the shivers of fear seizing her, she became aware of more. Of his thighs, clutched so tightly around her hips. Of his arms, pinioning her, to the floor.

And though she was shaking, she was tempted to reach up and touch his face. . . .

"Damn it! I had my chance! I might have caught him! If you hadn't opened that door—"

"Excuse me! I do apologize for thinking that any life—even yours—is valuable!"

"I told you to stay inside!"

"And I'm not in the military! I don't take orders!"

"This has nothing to do with the military! This has to do with common sense and living!"

He was so angry. She wanted to explode in return, except that she had been wrong, however nobly, and her teeth were chattering, and more than anything she simply wanted to stand. "Would you get up, please?"

He jumped up quickly, reaching down a hand to her. She didn't take it, but he grabbed her hand and pulled her to her feet anyway. "I'm taking a look around. Call the police. The emergency number."

Once again, he was gone. She dialed.

By the time he returned to the house, a patrol car was arriving. It had been a long day. The night promised to stretch into eternity.

When the first officers arrived, the younger one went out with Wes to survey the back while the older of the pair asked Reggie questions.

Within fifteen minutes, Sergeant Wiler, the detective in charge of Daphne's disappearance, arrived. Then they went through all the questions again.

Reggie made coffee.

The fingerprint men came and dusted every imaginable surface.

Wiler questioned Wes, but to Reggie's annoyance, the two seemed to have met already, and if they weren't exactly friends, they had acquired a wary respect for one another.

The bullet was dug out of her wall—along with a piece of the paneling.

"A .38," Wes said, looking at the chunk of wood and the bullet.

"Maybe ballistics can tell us a little bit more," Wiler said. He wagged a finger at Reggie. "Are you sure you're telling me everything, Miss Delaney?"

Reggie sighed. "Detective Wiler, if I could help in any way, don't you think that I would?" Wiler was annoyingly silent. "This could be an unrelated event, you know," she said with exasperation. "Maybe it was just a burglar."

"One who didn't *burgle* anything," Wes said lightly. He was leaning against the paneling at the rear of the kitchen, his arms crossed over his chest.

Wiler, a fortyish man with iron-gray hair, a hard, trim body and face to match, glanced his way quickly, then stared at Reggie. "Exactly."

Reggie threw up her hands. "Maybe it was a thief— one that we interrupted!"

"And maybe," Wes suggested softly, "there is something in particular here that someone wants—and hasn't managed to find as yet."

The sergeant frowned suddenly. Wiler had been staring at her strangely since he had arrived. He was seated at her breakfast table, and she was resting tiredly against the sink. He leaned toward her, his frown deepening.

"Just where were you this evening?"

"We went to dinner, Sergeant. We just went to dinner—"

"Dressed like that?"

Reggie stiffened, remembering that she was still in the garish red costume with fishnet stockings. No wonder they had all been staring at her. "It was a very late day," she said flatly.

One of the fingerprint men snickered, then quickly looked at his dusting.

"Maybe this particular thief knew that you were going to be out. Did you tell anyone you were going to dinner?"

"No," Reggie said. "No, just—"

Max. Max had known.

And Wes was thinking the same thing. She could tell by the way he was looking at her.

That was ridiculous. Absolutely ridiculous. Max would never hurt her, let alone shoot at her. Surely Wes knew that.

"*Just who,* Miss Delaney?" Wiler persisted.

"No one. I'm so tired, I really can't think," she said wearily.

"Maybe someone did know that you would be out."

Reggie pressed her temples between her thumb and forefinger. "Maybe. I don't know. But gentlemen, it has been a very long day, and I'm going to have another long day tomorrow. If you don't mind...?" She let the implication trail as politely as she could.

Wiler stood. "Well, we can keep a patrol going around the area for the night, I suppose. We'll see what we can find out with these prints, too. Let's hope that he—or she—doesn't come back!"

Reggie stiffened, some of her exhaustion dropping away as little tingles of fear seized her again.

Someone had been here.

Someone with a gun. And the police were just going to keep a car circling around the neighborhood.

Wes was staring at her again. Hard. With the same look of aggravated disbelief he had given her when she had thrown open the door in the hope that he was still alive despite the gunfire.

"There's no alarm on this house, is there?" Wes asked, frowning.

"This is not a crime-ridden city—" Reggie began.

"This is the twentieth century!" he responded irritably. He looked at Wiler. "It's all right. I'll stay."

Wiler nodded. "I'm sure you know your business, Colonel."

"Wait!" Reggie began, but Wiler was already rising; his men, with all their paraphernalia, were following him as he quickly strode to the door, talking all the while to Wes.

"I don't have the manpower for this sort of thing myself. Have you got a piece?"

"In my car."

"A permit? You are a civilian now, I take it."

"Yes, and yes, I have a permit," Wes told him.

"Wait!" Reggie tried again.

They might have all gone deaf. No one paid her the least heed. "Good night, Miss Delaney." Wiler suddenly stopped short in the doorway to wag a finger at her. "You take care, Miss Delaney. And when you think of something, you let me know!"

"Sergeant—"

"Somebody knows something here, and somebody had best start talking soon! Keep in touch," he warned over his shoulder.

Wes had followed him halfway down to his car, his hands on his hips, watching as Wiler's car—then the other three—churned into action and started down the drive. Then Wes went to his car, opened the passenger door and reached into the glove compartment.

Reggie didn't know anything about guns. Nothing. She'd never had to know anything about them—she had never wanted to know anything about them. She didn't know what it was that Wes carried, except that it was silver and sleek and compact. She felt cold just staring at it.

He walked up the steps, the long nose of the gun pointed downward. He held the weapon comfortably, like a man familiar with it.

He looked at her, his head cocked. "I know. You don't want me staying here."

She shook her head slowly. "I never said that."

"Well, I'm staying."

He was so stubborn. She smiled suddenly, wryly. "For your information, smarty-pants, I'm glad that you're staying. I was shot at this evening. I guess—"

"You guess what?"

"I guess that I might have been frightened if I knew I had to stay here alone tonight."

"That's sensible."

"And you weren't expecting it. People who dream up dinosaur characters can't be sensible, is that it?"

He stared at her, a slow smile curving his lips. "No, that isn't it at all."

"Oh!"

"Women who throw open doors when they hear shots exploding can't be expected to be very sensible," he told her.

"Next time I think you might be injured, I'll just let you bleed to death," she informed him in a lofty tone.

"Let's go inside."

Reggie turned and walked into her house. "Yes, come in, Mr. Blake. And please—you're always such a reticent man! Do make yourself at home."

She felt him behind her. Felt the warmth of his breath whispering over her nape. "I intend to, Miss Delaney. Trust me. I intend to."

* * *

Reggie didn't really mean to be rude; she was glad he was staying—glad that *someone* was with her, someone who didn't seem to be afraid in the least of violence.

If she was rude at that point, it was simply because she felt so awkward.

But Wesley Blake didn't make a bad houseguest. She told him that he didn't need to curl up on the sofa or anything, that there were three guest rooms on the second floor, the most comfortable being the upper corner room with the kind-size bed. But even saying the word *bed* to him brought a surprising rush of color to her cheeks and she turned away as she spoke.

"You'll have to excuse me," she murmured. "I have to change now. There's coffee or tea in the kitchen, beer in the fridge, and there's a bar in the family room. There's cheese in the drawer, crackers in the cabinets—"

"I'm all right," he told her. Then he smiled slightly. Her discomfort must have been obvious. "I'll be down here in the library. I saw rows of books and a television. I'm sure I can entertain myself."

She left him and hurried upstairs to her room and the private bath to the side of it.

At long last she stripped off the black net hose and the dance hall dress, making a mental note to drop it off at the front of the park for cleaning and return it to the show first thing in the morning. Naked, she stepped beneath the spray of the water.

As the warm, steaming water streamed over her, she felt each drop, each touch. And she was thinking about the man who was in her library, just yards away.

She had tousled his hair with dino-fingers.

She wondered what it would feel like to *really* touch him. Short and sandy, his hair would be crisp and rich beneath her fingertips. And the texture of his face. A face so handsome and masculine, the rugged face of a western hero, perhaps.

Where the water touched her, she imagined his hands. Rivulets poured over her shoulders and dripped between her breasts. And water fell softly and in cascades against her navel and trickled in a hot burst slowly between her legs.

She gasped in dismay at her thoughts and closed her eyes tightly.

Was he really the first decent man who had walked into her life in so long? Had she forgotten love so quickly?

No to both questions, she defended herself. She knew a number of fine men, they'd just never...

Never touched this longing, this need, inside her.

And she had never forgotten love. Neither the love she had felt for Caleb, nor the pain of his loss.

But he had been dead for nearly three years. And like it or not, Wesley Blake had awakened things in her that had not been set at rest when she had buried Caleb.

Maybe he had even awakened new things; she had been so much younger when she had fallen in love with Caleb, and the emotions, the sensations, had taken time to develop and grow.

Yet with this man...

"My Lord, I must be horrible!" she whispered. The water thundered in her ears in reply. *He is no one in my life!* she wanted to cry.

He had just come for Max. He would stay until the trouble had been cleared up. And then he would go back to his own life.

Did it matter? Wasn't that for the best?

She set her face beneath the spray of water and tried dully to remind herself that Wes was in her house because someone had come in here today. Someone had violated her privacy.

Someone had shot at her, had just missed her head by inches.

And that someone might have taken aim against her again if Wes hadn't flattened her to the ground—angrily. Despite that sexy smile, he also had a way of speaking in an unequivocal tone, as if he was explaining things to a toddler.

He gave orders. He expected them to be followed.

She turned off the water with a jerk and stepped from the shower. She quickly wrapped herself in the soft pink well-worn terry robe that hung from the hook on the bathroom door.

What a thing to wear downstairs! she chastised herself. First he was out with a red-draped hussy. Now he'd find himself staying with a hausfrau!

She was tempted, tempted beyond belief, to dig through her closet and find something more attractive, something . . . alluring.

She clamped down hard on her teeth and assured herself that even if her thoughts were running to the base side, she was civilized and grown-up, capable of controlling such insane urges.

He had his annoying ways about him. And he had his appeal. Yet even while insisting that he stay, he had been above board about it all. The man had no intention of seducing her.

Would he even want to?

She drew a hard knot in the belt of her robe, pushed back the damp wings of her hair and looked at her reflection in the mirror.

Squeaky clean. That was the best that could be said for her. She didn't dare think any longer. She hurried down the stairs.

She could hear the news playing on the television from the library. She ducked her head in quickly.

He had heard her, it seemed. She had padded down the stairway in barefoot silence, but he had heard her. He was looking up, waiting for her to appear. He was comfortably seated on the big leather chesterfield sofa, a Robert Ludlum paperback in his hands, a mug of something hot on the coffee table before him—and the gun in the center of the table.

"Hello," he said, after having waited for her to speak.

She nodded, stepping into the room. It was her house, she reminded herself.

"Are you all set? There are towels in the closet in the bath. I was just thinking, there are three rooms up there, but the bed is only put together in that last one. My housekeeper doesn't like to keep sheets on beds when they're not in use and she does such a wonderful job that I let her really have the run of the place. It is the most comfortable room—"

"I'll be fine."

She nodded again. She winced then, looking at the gun. "Does that have to be there?"

"It has to be in reach."

"Guns are just so—deadly."

He shook his head. "A gun itself is a tool. *People* are deadly—not guns."

"Well," she murmured awkwardly. "It's late. I guess I'm going up."

"I'm really sorry," he told her softly. There was such a curious light in those gold eyes. They touched her. They saw something in her.

Oh, God, please don't let him know the way I'm feeling! she thought in panic. He wouldn't understand. No one would understand. I don't even understand!

But it wasn't that.

When she had stood him up, he had been angry. When he wanted his way for his own purpose, he was going to get it.

But she was uncomfortable now, and he knew it, and he was truly sorry for it.

"If you think I don't want you here, that I wish you'd go home, you're wrong. I appreciate the fact that you're staying. I like living."

"Do you?"

"Of course."

His smile deepened, his lashes lowered slightly. "That's good to hear. Go on. Get some sleep. You will have lots of long days to come."

"You're sure you're all right? You'll find everything?"

"I'm fine. Good night."

"Good night."

Reggie ran up the stairs to her room, closed the door and catapulted onto her bed. She lay on her back, her fingers closing around the spread, her heart seeming to beat thousands of beats in a matter of seconds.

Think! Think of something else! Think of someone else. Think of a new puppet, a new song, a new character, think of Max...

Think of Caleb.

But neither ghosts nor any creatures of the imagination would come to her now. She lay there wretchedly in the darkness and thought of the man downstairs.

Why couldn't he have been an ancient old widower?

He was a widower, she remembered. That was one of the reasons she had assumed he would be old.

So who lay in his past? What ghost did he conjure in moments like this?

What woman had touched his sandy hair in truth, stretched her fingers over the broad expanse of his chest, lain beside that rugged bronze flesh....

She groaned softly and turned, burying her face in her pillow. Come, sleep! Please. But sleep eluded her for a long time.

Long past the moments when she heard the quiet sound of his footsteps on the stairs. Long past the time when she heard him enter the far guest room.

Long, long past the time when she heard the water running in the shower, heard it stop.

Heard the creak of the bed.

Heard...silence.

Then, thankfully, somewhere along the line, she slept.

Until she woke to the startling sound of an explosion in the street.

Chapter 7

The sound brought her leaping instantly to her feet. She switched on the overhead lamp, desperate for light, and raced into the hallway. "Wesley!"

He was up, too. Standing just outside his doorway. He had slipped his pants on. His chest was naked, taut, rippling with bronze muscle in the glare of the light.

His hair was tousled, his expression irritated.

But Reggie took those things in slowly. She ran the length of the hallway, leaping right into his arms. He held her while her teeth chattered and she gasped out, "Gunfire, downstairs! Didn't you hear it?"

He sighed. With exasperation. "It was a car, Reggie."

"What?"

"It was a car." He caught her arm and drew her into the guest room, to the window. From the second floor, she could see the length of the street. Far down the scarcely inhabited street, her neighbors' teenage son was out with friends, laughing—so it appeared—at the antics of a prized '57 Chevy.

Reggie exhaled a slow, wavering sigh. She'd been on her toes. She sank to her feet.

She became very aware of Wes, standing silently beside her. His arm just touching the fabric of her robe. Heat seeming to emanate from his body.

The hair on his chest was almost white. The bronze color of sleek flesh rippled beneath it.

"I—" she murmured.

"You!" He was suddenly wagging a finger at her. "Let's say that had been a gunshot. Reggie, you don't turn on a light!"

"But it was dark—"

"That's right, Reggie. No one can see you in the dark, or aim at you in the dark! Got it?"

"I'm sorry! I wasn't in the military!"

"That's common sense," he said flatly. "And another thing—you don't start shrieking. You stay silent, and you stay down, understand?"

Her teeth grated. She saluted him sharply. She sank into her sweetest, softest Southern accent. "Hey, I'm just a dumb old dinosaur dreamer—"

She gasped when she found her upper arms caught by his hands, her body drawn to his. Nothing but thin strips of terry separated her bare flesh from the hot naked length of his.

Hot, living, pulsing, naked length . . .

Hazel-gold eyes blazed into her, amused . . . intense.

"Dumb, my hind side!" he exclaimed harshly. "Reggie, damn you, I'm not trying to come off as G.I.

Joe here. It's just that you are in danger. And you have to think, all right?''

She was watching his mouth move. The movement came first to her mind.

Then the words.

"Reggie!" He gave her a little shake.

She nodded. "No lights. No screams." She was trembling. She didn't know if she was frightened of having to walk away from him and go to her room alone. Or if she was frightened of staying.

"Good," he said softly. He released her arms. "Are you afraid?"

"No," she said. "Yes. I don't know." She took a step away. "Good night, again." She forced herself to walk down the hallway without turning back, even though she knew he watched her. Watched her the entire distance, standing outside the doorway of the guest room.

She stepped into her room. She started to close the door. Then she left it open.

He could say what he wanted to say. She wanted him within screaming distance.

No, she wasn't afraid....

She forced herself to lie down. Her heart seemed to be pounding at a thousand beats a minute again. But he was just down the hall. He would never let anything happen to her; if nothing else, she felt secure about that.

She hardly knew him.

But she felt that she knew him very well.

Oh, dear Lord! She was so tempted to get up and walk down the hall. He would understand. He was angry when she risked things, but he would understand that she just didn't want to stay here. He might be sleeping. That would be fine. She could take her pillow and curl up in the armchair and she might get some sleep that way.

But she knew damned well that she didn't want to sleep in an armchair.

She suspected that she would want far more than security if she were to walk down the hallway.

Caleb! she thought desperately, trying to draw upon some sanity.

But evoking his name did not help. She had begun to let his memory, to let the good and the bad, the laughter, the love and the pain, come to rest. She had never, in any way, betrayed him in life or in death. Max was right. She needed more than the park. Needed more than dreams.

She had never wanted more....

Until tonight.

Her heartbeat should be slowing by now.

The fear was fading. The sound of the explosion had died away on the night air.

Her heartbeat continued to pound. Pulsing. Sending the blood cascading through her body. Waking every nerve and fiber of her.

Indeed. She had never felt quite so wide awake in the middle of the night before.

She had never felt quite so...

Wanting?

Yes, she wanted . . . something.

Wes.

Damn those kids with that car! He'd almost been asleep. Almost.

Well, all right, not really.

But he might have been able to go to sleep if the fool car hadn't backfired, if Reggie hadn't come racing down the hallway and into his arms.

If he hadn't touched her.

Now, he was staring at the ceiling in the muted darkness, seeing nothing but the pale sheen of the paint. No, seeing everything there, as if the white paint that caught a dim glow of moonlight were a canvas and he could play images there, as if he were a projector and the ceiling were a screen.

He still wondered how someone who resembled Max, a man, could be so beautiful. So completely feminine. So alluring. In no matter what manner of dress he conjured her. She had so much dignity in her red business suit. She'd been sleek, sharp, determined. A worthy adversary to any man, he was certain, he thought, a curl forming in the corner of his lip. But he couldn't stay focused on that red suit.

Her clothing seemed to slip away.

He was thinking next of the brilliant red dance-hall costume, and how she had looked across the table from him at the restaurant.

Lobster shells flying.

But even that image wouldn't remain.

The one that came again and again was of Reggie in the costume shop. The dinosaur outfit in her hands.

Tall, slim, in the muted maroon bra and panties, so much of the woman visible and so much of the woman, all of the woman, beautiful and sensual. Her build was slim, but just slightly muscled. Her calves were beautifully shaped, giving her long, tempting legs. Hips flared just slightly, evocatively. Her waist seemed as trim as Scarlett O'Hara's, and her breasts...

He groaned and closed his eyes tightly against the images. For a moment he marveled at the way she had made him feel. Even the frustration was good.

The hunger was even better. Oh, he'd been hungry before. He'd wanted women before. He had had women before.

But it had never mattered before. Not in the long years since Shelley.

He opened his eyes again. He still didn't like to remember.

Better to concentrate on the woman down the hallway.

Yeah, even on breasts.

They had been full and beautiful, rising over the lacy maroon of the bra. That lace had barely covered the darkened crests of her nipples. He'd have loved to reach out and touch. He hadn't even been introduced to her then.

Excuse me, Miss Delaney, but this is making me insane. The mystery, the longing. Could I move this wisp of lace for a minute just to see . . .

He ground his teeth. She was Max's sister.

Right. And like Max, she was thirty-three years old.

The hell with Max.

Max had no place in his fantasies.

But in a way, he did. Wes tried to remember all that Max had told him about his sister, Regina. Why had he never been curious about her before?

Shelley had been in his life.

And someone else had been in Regina's life. Caleb. That had been his name. She had been engaged for years to a fellow named Caleb. Engaged. She had never married him.

Why?

Had she been too attached to her own name? Max's name? The Delaney name?

She had loved the man. The way Max had talked, they had really been a team. Then something had happened. An accident. He tried hard to concentrate. Yes, it had been a drunk driver. Now he remembered it all, remembered Max telling him. The man had been hit by a drunk driver. He hadn't died immediately. That had taken time.

It had been awhile ago, though. Several years, he was fairly certain.

What about her life now?

Well, she didn't like Rick Player, that much had been pretty obvious.

Good. That said she had some sense—even if she did turn on lights when bullets might be flying. Player was smooth. He was the type most women seemed to fall for. Reggie disliked the man. She hid it the best she could, but Wes knew she disliked him.

Wes suddenly heard something from the hall. A sound, barely discernible, but there nonetheless. No one had come in the house from the outside, he was certain.

It had to be Reggie.

He pushed up somewhat, leaning against his pillow and the bedstead, watching the door. Every muscle tightened, but he didn't make a move. His gun was sitting on the small antique oak night table at the side of the bed. If he needed it, he could reach it.

But intuition assured him that he wasn't going to need it.

Then she appeared in the doorway. She was still in the terry robe. Her dark hair was loose, disheveled, free around her shoulders. Moonlight played upon it beautifully, beams cascading over it whitely.

"Wes? Are you sleeping?" she queried softly. Her fingers were long, elegant and delicate against the door frame. He wondered what her fingers would feel like against his skin.

"No."

He hadn't needed to answer her. The moon gave enough brightness to the room that they could see each other. He was almost sitting up. Sheets drawn to his waist, chest bare, eyes open.

Awake, and aware. In every sense of the word. A rising sense of heat seemed to enter the room right along with her. She stood at the foot of the bed. She hadn't dressed to be a temptress, he thought.

Not consciously.

And yet . . .

She couldn't have been more so. The frayed terry was so soft looking, the pink such a compelling color on her. The V fell open just to the rise of her breasts, and he could remember that rise when it had been so tightly clad in the maroon lace of her bra. Just as he had been enticed to see more then, he wanted to see more now. To see, to touch. He ached to touch. He didn't dare move. Tension was knotting his every muscle.

Desire would soon make a tent of the sheet.

"I—I didn't want to be alone," she said. She was waiting for something. From him. An invitation? He was willing to give one!

But only if her feelings were the right ones . . .

"You don't want to be alone, or you want to be with someone?" he said, watching her eyes in the darkness. They were so large. So luminous. "There is a difference. Which is it?"

He could tell that she wanted to lie. She moistened her lips to speak. He watched the movement of her tongue and lips.

"I—don't know," she murmured softly. "Is there such a difference?"

He pushed himself farther up with his hands. His knees bent as he rested his elbows on them, watching her. "A tremendous difference. Are you afraid to be alone?"

"No. Yes." She swallowed hard. "Yes, but that's not why I'm here."

"Then you want to be with someone."

She hesitated. "It's not that simple."

"I hope not."

"You're not making things very easy."

"They shouldn't be easy."

Maybe he pressed it a bit too far. Her body was tensing, and she was about to turn away, but he caught hold of her hand. In the moonlight her eyes were liquid. It had cost her a lot to come here. Maybe he was being ruthless.

He had to be.

"Do you just want a warm body?" he demanded.

She tugged hard to free her hand. "Let go! If you would—"

"Answer me. Did you just want a warm body?"

She tugged harder. "No! Damn it—let me go. I knew this was a mistake. You want—"

"Yes, I want!" he told her roughly. Still maintaining his grip on her, he cast his covers aside and came to his feet. Her eyes were locked with his, yet she was aware that he had been completely naked beneath the sheet, and she was struggling to keep her eyes on his face. She still fought his hold. He tightened his fingers relentlessly around her wrist and drew her hand to his body, forcing her palm against his chest. "I want," he whispered, towering over her, his breath teasing her forehead and the soft strands of hair there. "I've lain here all night and thought of nothing but what I want. But I don't play warm flesh, and I don't do body doubles for any man. So there is a big difference to me in the reasons you might have come. Not just so that you're not alone. And not just so that you're with someone. Be here to be with me."

She inhaled a ragged sob. "I've never done anything like this before in my entire life. And now you're making fun of me. If you don't want—"

He let out a soft, swift expletive. "Lady, haven't you listened to a thing I've said?" To emphasize his point, he brought her palm against his heart. She felt the giant pulse of it. She nearly jumped, trying to withdraw her hand, but he wasn't going to allow her to. He wasn't going to give an inch. Her eyes were even wider than before. Greener, emerald in the moonlight. The tousled jet tendrils of her hair were a sensual frame to the beauty of her face. The fuzzy pink robe was coming loose. The V at her breasts was spreading. He brought their hands from his chest to hers. He laid his palm at the valley there, and felt the thunder of her heart.

He smiled.

With his free hand, he caught her body at the base of her spine and brought her hard against him. "I want you, Regina. Don't ever doubt that I want you."

He emphasized the point once again. This time he brought her hand to his hip, then led her lower. He brought her fingers around the hard shaft of his manhood. A shudder ripped through him and he rued his own determination as the longing constricted into something painful. Her mouth formed an O and a soft gasp escaped her. He swore hoarsely, threading his fingers through her hair and lifting her face to his. "I want you. I've lain here all night imagining you. With and without clothing. I've never encountered a woman I wanted so desperately. But I don't want you because you're afraid, and most of all, I don't want you if you're going to jump up in the morning and be horrified and want to pretend that nothing ever happened. Understand?"

Miraculously, her fingers were still upon him. That touch. That simple touch. Had he wanted her so damn badly, really, that just this subtle—and scarcely willing!—caress could send him over some brink?

No! He wanted to make love to her. Wanted to make it the best night she'd known in her life.

Had he pushed it too far again? Would she refuse to play by his rules?

He gave her a slight shake. "Understand?"

Lightning fires were shooting through his body. In about two seconds he wouldn't give a damn if she understood or not, if she had listened to a word he had said. The want was going to be need. He would have to have her, just as he would have to breathe in the moments to come.

She blinked. To his amazement a soft smile curled her lip. "I have to jump up in the morning. I have to go to work."

He lowered his face to hers. His lips hovered just above hers as he spoke. "You can go to work, Reggie. I'll take you. But you can't pretend. You can't look through me in the hallway. And I won't lie to anyone about this."

She didn't answer. He didn't care anymore. He had put everything on the line.

And her mouth was there. Just below his. The mouth that had been made to be kissed.

And he was going to kiss it.

He did. He covered it with the fullness of his own. Teased her lips with the tip of his tongue. Forced his way past them. Delved deep, drank deep. Felt the warmth of her mouth encompass and sheath the thrust of his tongue.

And felt the lightning fires searing through him again. He was ablaze, a mass of tension and desire, pulsing beats that desperately sought a release. And she was still touching him. Bringing him closer and closer to an explosive brink.

His lips broke from hers. Wet, liquid, slightly puffed and so damp from their kiss, her lips were ever so desirable. But he wanted more. He lifted her hair and touched his lips to her shoulders.

He slipped his hands beneath the shoulders of her robe and pushed the robe to the floor.

And like him, she was naked.

Naked and beautiful. Her breasts, the breasts he had fantasized about for so long, seemed a greater marvel than any picture he could conjure. They were full and firm with generous, dusky rose areolae and nipples. His hand instantly sought the fullness of her right breast. His thumb rolled and teased the nipple.

He bent down to taste the fullness of it.

She cried out softly, arching against him. A searing band seemed to stretch across his loin as he touched her, as he drank so deeply from her. He wanted to give her so much.

And for the moment, to give was to take.

He lifted her into his arms, casting her down on the bed, quickly crawling atop her. Her eyes were on his all the while. He needed her so badly.

His hands moved swiftly over the length of her, caressing, brushing her flesh, bringing warmth, evocative, arousing. He kissed and caressed her breasts, stroked her thighs and ran his palm firmly along her hip and the outer thigh. Pressing into the encompassing softness of the bed, he parted her thighs with the weight of his body. The scent of her was sweet and as tempting as a siren's song. He buried his face against her throat, kissed her earlobe, teased the pulse with his tongue.

With a massive shift, a sudden movement, he was inside her. A soft gasp noted her surprise at his abrupt invasion. A deep shuddering seized her as he tried to hold still, to take time, but she was warm and wet and sheathed him so sweetly, adding temptation, promising relief to the hunger. He groaned, sinking into her. She was small and tight. He thought fleetingly that it must have been forever since she had made love.

He whispered something to her. Words that made no sense. He kissed and nuzzled her ear and she gasped again, her arms circling him, her long, slender legs doing the same. The welcoming movement on her part sent new sensations blazing through him. A fire that could not be quenched. He abandoned all thoughts of gentleness to the moonlight and the night, and set free the pulse of longing and passion that had seized him from the beginning.

She was accepting the onslaught of his beat, of his hungry rhythm. Then she moved. Fluid, sweet. Her back arching, her hips rotating. Taking him, accepting him. Holding, stroking, with the tight clench of her body. Bringing him higher and higher, racing toward a peak. Fire burned inside him. Climax exploded upon him and he jerked, tightened, thrust hard and harder. A searing seed spilled from him, filling her.

A soft gasp escaped her as she tightened, holding tight to him. He drew away. Her eyes were glazed. He had given her so little. And she had given him so much.

He couldn't leave it that way. She started to speak but he caught her lips. Kissed her slowly. Gently. Explored. Teased. Demanded with his mouth. Took it away. Drank deeply of her lips once again.

Then he began to shift down her body. Catching her breasts. Taking his time loving them both. So slowly. So tenderly.

She didn't seem to realize that they had barely begun. And she was whispering awkwardly to him.

He slipped his hand beneath the small of her back, lifting the smooth ivory plane of her stomach to his lips. He brushed the flesh with his tongue. Ran his lips across it. Delved into her navel with his kiss.

"You were really—"

"What?"

She gasped. He was running his tongue, wet, slick, along her upper thigh. Gently forcing her knees apart once again.

"You—"

She broke off, again gasping. He breathed against the very center of feminine desire. Touched so lightly with the tip of his tongue.

Delved so deeply.

She choked out something, digging into the bedding. Protesting. Not protesting. It didn't matter. He could feel the sudden soaring of the passion within her, and he wouldn't have released her then, wouldn't have granted her quarter, had she screamed for mercy. For as it was, each twist and sweet undulation of her body sent the raw edge of desire flaming within him once again. It grew to become an agony. A pulsing that strained and contorted his muscle and loin, near bursting. But he waited. Calmly taking his leisure of her beautiful flesh, waited until she rocked against him. Pleading...

And then he rose above her.

That time, it was she who gasped and sobbed softly, pulsing against him in a whirlwind, tightening, shuddering, straining, then collapsing below him while he held her, taking his own release more slowly, only after she had found hers. Then, drenched, seeking to breathe again at a rational pace, holding her still, he let her lie quietly beside him, her hand upon his belly, her head upon his chest.

"Wes—"

He pressed his fingers against her lips.

"Thank you," he said softly.

"I was horrible—"

"Horrible? I'm not sure that I'll be able to stand it when you are good!"

"No, no, I mean, coming in here like this, tonight. I don't even know you. Not really."

"Correction. I think you know me very well."

She pressed a kiss against his chest, and he felt her smile. "Parts of you!"

He stroked the ink-black hair that lay damp and tangled over him. "I gave you fair warning," he told her. "I won't let you leap away, and I won't let you pretend that nothing happened here."

"Everything happened here," she murmured. Then she pushed against him. Max's sister was very beautiful and an incredible woman. She made love with the same passion with which she lived.

"I didn't mean that the way that it sounded. I mean, I don't expect anything from you. I just don't—I don't make a habit of doing things like this. It just seemed right. You were just so—"

"Ungodly sexy?" he suggested.

"Oh, no, it—"

"I'm not ungodly sexy?" he added, disappointed.

It brought a smile to her lips. Those lips that still seemed made for kissing.

"Oh, you are sexy."

"Ungodly sexy."

"All right—ungodly sexy!" She laughed, but then her laughter faded and she added softly, "But it was more. Much more. I don't know if I can make you understand. I don't know if I can make myself understand."

He lifted a hand, smoothing some of the hair from her face. "You're pretty ungodly sexy yourself," he told her huskily. "And if you hadn't come down that hall tonight, I might have died of the longing for you."

"No one dies from longing," she said.

"Want to bet?"

Yes, hers were lips made for kissing, and he kissed them again, his hand cupping her nape and bringing her face to his.

Then, while he kissed her, he let his hands start to roam again. Even as he kissed her, her eyes widened. Some sound gurgled in her throat. His lips rose above hers and she whispered, "We can't—"

"Why can't we?"

"We just—"

"Can," he assured her. "We can."

And he began to make love to her in earnest once again.

She was a mistress of fantasy. A creator of magic. And this night, she had most certainly created some fantastic magic for him.

There would be no denials. He was firm about that. Yet he knew that the daylight would come, and that it would mean different things to both of them. He wouldn't let her walk away.

But still . . .

He wanted to hold on to the night. To hold on as passionately and fiercely as he could, for as long as he could.

Nights might be frequent.

Sometimes, even love was easy.
But magic...
Magic was always rare.

Chapter 8

"It makes no sense!" Max said. They were in the large meeting room above the entry cave. She hadn't thought to say anything to Max about the intruder.

Wes had.

But he had forgotten to mention to her that he was going to tell Max, and when her brother had summoned her to the room and she had discovered Max and Wes sitting at the table and staring at her, she had felt as guilty as a two-year-old stealing candy. She'd even forgotten why Wes had stayed with her in the first place. Color had filled her face and she stood there staring at the two of them. Then Max had finally spoken. "Damn it, Reggie, you should have called me immediately."

The intruder. They were talking about the intruder. Wes had said he wouldn't lie, but at least he hadn't come running to Max to tell him that she had come to his bedroom the night before.

What would Max's reaction have been? Anger? Damn it, Wes, I call you for help, and you seduce my sister? Or amusement? Hell, I have been telling Reggie to get a life!

But Wes had done nothing so drastic—he had told Max about the intruder, and she had managed to sit down with the two of them. She hadn't talked much at first; she hadn't needed to. Wes explained about coming back from dinner and hearing the back door close. He told about the shots, too, and she was grateful that he omitted the part about her throwing the door open in the midst of the shooting. "It makes no sense!" Max said then, shaking his head and staring at Reggie. "Why would someone break into your house? I can't seem to make two and two equal four."

"Maybe two and two don't equal four," Reggie said. She looked at her brother. She couldn't look at Wes without feeling the color rise to her cheeks again. She wasn't trying to deny things. She just didn't dare think about them.

"Max, maybe there was just a sneak thief in my house. I told Wiler last night that it was possible someone just decided to rob the place."

"Right. And a casual robber shot at Wes, and then at you when Wes went after him."

"Sure. Shooting kept us from coming after him, right?"

Max sighed and stared at her.

Wes spoke up. "They just happened to decide to rob your house after all this time?"

"Coincidences do happen," Reggie said stubbornly, still looking at her brother. She sighed with exasperation. "Maybe some hood has been watching the place and realized that I live alone, and maybe even realized that I don't have an alarm—"

"That has to be fixed," Max said.

"Immediately," Wes agreed. They were looking at each other and discussing her as if she was a child.

Well, all right, maybe she did need to have an alarm installed.

"Think it can be done today?" Max asked Wes.

"I'm sure Wiler can see that it's done."

"But will he?"

"Hey, hey! Both of you, I'm still here, remember?"

They stared at her patiently.

"I can't have an alarm put in today, Max. First off, I need to be a dinosaur again. And you're still short a Patricia in the saloon show. Niles just told me that Mrs. O'Halloran from the main costume shop isn't sure if she'll return. Max, I'm the only one who can fill in for all these empty bodies. I can't sit at my house and wait."

Max tapped his pencil on his desk. "Diana will go wait in your place. She won't mind."

Diana was one of Max's friends. She worked in the art department. They had been dating since a month or so after his divorce. Actually, she had been a friend of Reggie's first, so it was hard for Reggie to come up with an excuse why Diana couldn't wait in her place.

"All right, Reggie?" Max asked.

"Yes, it's fine," she agreed.

But Max was frowning again. "Actually, I don't think you should stay out there alone even with an alarm. Not the way things have been happening."

"Max, I don't have the energy or the stamina to try to move out now!" she protested. "I'm putting in way too many hours—"

"The hours won't mean anything to anyone if something happens to you, Reggie."

"I can't—"

"I don't want you alone!"

For the moment, they had both forgotten Wes, having gotten into one of the squabbles they'd always managed to get into. But then Wes spoke up again. Softly. But his words quickly caught their attention.

"I can stay at Reggie's," he said. He leaned across the polished table, his bronze hands with their neat, blunt-cut nails stretched out before him. "I stayed out there last night. I can stay until this thing is over."

"I—I—" Reggie began. She was coloring. Despite a magnificent effort not to blush, she was reddening. She was staring at his hands. She shouldn't be doing that. Staring at his hands made her remember the way they had felt on her.

The way they could feel again . . .

She was strangling. "I wouldn't d-dream of putting you out," she managed to say. He stared at her. Flatly. Coldly. It did sound as if she was trying to deny things. Damn him! She was pleading with her eyes. She didn't want to deny things. She just didn't want to clunk her brother on the head with the truth.

"Oh, I don't think it would put me out too much," he replied dryly.

GET 4 BOOKS

FREE

Return this card, and we'll send you 4 brand-new Silhouette Intimate Moments® novels, absolutely FREE! We'll even pay the postage both ways!

We're making you this offer to introduce you to the benefits of the Silhouette Reader Service™: free home delivery of brand-new romance novels, months before they're available in stores, AND at a saving of 43¢ apiece compared to the cover price!

Accepting these 4 free books places you under no obligation to buy. You may cancel at any time, even just after receiving your free shipment. If you do not cancel, every month, we'll send 6 more Silhouette Intimate Moments® novels and bill you just $2.96* apiece—that's all!

Yes! Please send me my 4 free Silhouette Intimate Moments® novels, as explained above.

Name

Address   Apt.

City   State   ZIP

245 CIS AGL3

*Terms and prices subject to change without notice. Sales tax applicable in N.Y. Offer limited to one per household and not valid to current Silhouette Intimate Moments® subscribers. All orders subject to approval.

© 1990 Harlequin Enterprises Limited.

PRINTED IN CANADA

Get 4 Books FREE

SEE BACK OF CARD FOR DETAILS

FREE MYSTERY GIFT

We will be happy to send you a free bonus gift along with your free books! To request it, please check here and mail this reply card promptly!

Thank you!

BUSINESS REPLY CARD

FIRST CLASS MAIL   PERMIT NO. 717   BUFFALO, NY

POSTAGE WILL BE PAID BY ADDRESSEE

SILHOUETTE READER SERVICE
3010 WALDEN AVE
P O BOX 1867
BUFFALO NY 14240-9952

NO POSTAGE
NECESSARY
IF MAILED
IN THE
UNITED STATES

DETACH ALONG DOTTED LINE AND MAIL TODAY! – DETACH ALONG DOTTED LINE AND MAIL TODAY! – DETACH ALONG DOTTED LINE AND MAIL TODAY! – DETACH ALONG DOTTED LINE AND MAIL TODAY!

"Can you?" Max said. "I'd be grateful. I'd feel that Reggie was definitely safe with you."

"Hey." He lifted his hands idly, staring at Reggie. "Regina's house, the hotel suite. Doesn't make much difference."

"Thanks!" She heard herself murmur. But Max was too worried to notice anything in her tone. "I'll call Diana—Wes, give Wiler a call and ask him to call whoever he thinks does the best job in the area. Hyer's Corporation takes care of the park, but I don't know how they work with private residences, and Reggie's house is pretty far out of the city."

Wes stood. He was in jeans that hugged his form very nicely, and his hair was still damp—he must have showered when he came into the office.

He hadn't showered at her house. They'd woken so late. But they hadn't gone to sleep until late. She'd been sound asleep when he nudged her, a cup of coffee in his hand. "We've got to get moving. Park opens in an hour." He'd already been dressed, and for a moment, she'd felt ridiculously shy again, naked, tousled, with him dressed, his hair combed, even his socks and shoes on.

But she hadn't had time to think about it. She'd leaped up, spilling the coffee, then pausing as he pulled her into the crook of his arm. "Woah! Take a second! Drink the coffee—it will help. Promise. I tried it already."

And so, in the crook of his arm, she'd swallowed the coffee and spoke shyly. "Thanks! It is good." But then she had moved out of his arm and run down the hallway and into a quick shower that was, at best, a promise of things to come. Then she'd hopped into black jeans and a short-sleeved tailored white cotton shirt, whisked her lashes with a brush of mascara and come running down the stairs with her comb tearing through the wild disaster of her hair.

Wes had been quiet while they drove to the park, so quiet that she felt walls building between them. But then his hand had fallen over hers when they reached the park, and he'd given her one of those smiles that could eclipse the heart.

"See you later?"

"Well, of course—"

"No, I meant, see you later?" And those golden eyes had blazed into hers with such a startling fire that she had felt a rush of warmth stir her cheeks. And she had nodded emphatically, but when she wanted to get out of the car, he pulled her back.

"Was it good to be with someone?"

"Yes!" she had whispered.

"With me?"

The fire had been spreading through her. Nighttime had been so easy. Daylight was always hard.

"I never ask for a lot. Just honesty," he'd told her.

"Yes! With you!"

He'd released her arm, and she'd fled past him through the dinosaur caves, waving to the morning guard. They had managed to arrive nearly thirty minutes before opening time.

In her office she had been barraged with phone calls.

And then Max had summoned her.

And now Wes was staring at her and she was having a hard time meeting his gaze. Honesty. That was all he wanted. But honesty was sometimes the hardest thing to give.

Her lashes lowered over her eyes. She found herself nervously moistening her lips with her tongue.

"I won't be putting you out, will I, Reggie?" Wes asked politely. There was such an edge to the question.

Surely Max would notice it. But he didn't. "Oh, Reggie will be thrilled, I'm sure," her brother answered cheerfully for her.

Wes set his palms on the polished table and leaned down, looking into her eyes. "Well, Reggie?" His eyes could burn when he wanted them to. "Is that true? Will you be just thrilled?"

"I—I'll be happy to have you there, of course," she murmured primly.

He pushed away from the desk in disgust. She clenched her teeth, wishing she could make him understand and suddenly feeling desolate because she had exasperated him so badly.

But he was already leaving the room, walking to the door with long strides. Before he left he turned and waved a finger at Reggie. "Don't leave without me."

"But I—"

"I've got to leave the park for awhile today. I'll be back for you. Even with Diana and the alarm people at your house, don't leave *here* without me. Got it?"

His tone was sharp. Commanding. She wanted to tell him that she'd damn well do what she felt like doing, but she was suddenly certain that if she did, he'd come striding into the boardroom and wrench her from her feet and have it out then and there.

And she wasn't ready to have anything out.

"After the show, I'll be in the main costume shop trying to sort things out," she said stiffly.

"Good."

He left. She realized that Max was watching her intently. She turned on her brother.

"I don't know exactly what his position was in the military, but he sounds like a damned drill sergeant!" she said irritably.

"He was an intelligence officer," Max said briefly. "He decided to leave after the Iraqi war because he has such a length of plate in the one leg that he can foretell the weather with it. He knows what he's doing. Thank God you're being agreeable to having him at the house!"

"Yes, well..." Reggie murmured, rising quickly herself.

"Reggie!"

"Yes?"

"Why the hell didn't you call me last night?"

She shrugged. She didn't want to admit that, with Wes there, she didn't even think of it. "Max, I'm sorry. If I had called you, what good would it have done? You and Wes could have just run around outside together."

"Thank God he didn't leave you! But then, Wes never would have left anyone in circumstances like that."

"How noble," she said in a soft grating tone.

Max shrugged. "Maybe he irritates you, Reggie, but his wife used to say that he was the last of the cavaliers. I think that maybe she was right, in a way."

"His—wife?"

Max arched a brow. "Yes, wife. The woman that one marries."

"But you told me that he was a widower—"

"He's a widower now, but obviously he wasn't always," Max said, curiosity touching his eyes.

Reggie suddenly found herself wanting to stay when she had been in such a big hurry only moments before. "What happened to his wife?"

He sighed softly, reflectively. "She died of cancer. They both knew she had it for several years. They lived with it, doing the best they could. It's all that any of us can do, isn't it?"

He stared at her hard then. Neither of them was thinking about Shelley Blake at the moment.

We do the best we can . . . He had told her that once before. Yes, that was what they had done with Caleb.

There had been nothing else to do.

"So you knew—Shelley?" she asked.

Max nodded. "Sure. Wes was military for a long time. He didn't get all that much time off. Shelley was with him several of the times when we met in San Francisco."

"What was she like?"

"Soft, blond. An angel," Max murmured. "She had the most beautiful smile. I don't think I've ever met a woman more feminine. Ethereal. Her hair was almost silver, it was so light. She was gracious and charming. Even when she knew she was going to die."

"It sounds as if you were just a little bit in love yourself," Reggie said, wondering why she should feel this sudden sense of resentment. She wasn't a mean person. She should have been delighted that Wesley's wife had been so wonderful.

It was just that she was wondering how she compared.

What did it matter? Poor Shelley was gone. Just like Caleb.

But Wes had loved Shelley. What would he be like with a woman he loved?

"No, I was just thinking . . ." Max said.

"What?"

"I don't know. I was thinking about all the differences between Shelley and Daphne. Want to hear something terrible? There were a lot of days when I wondered how somebody like Shelley could die—when someone like Daphne enjoyed such wonderful good health. It didn't seem fair then. And now . . ."

"Daphne might very well be just fine," Reggie reminded her brother hastily.

"Maybe. I hope so. I really do."

A soft silence fell between them. Then a phone rang somewhere down the hall, and Reggie cleared her throat. "I do have to go play dinosaur," she told him.

"Hey, don't feel too bad. I have to be David Diplodocus for the four o'clock appearance," he said glumly.

"Hey! David's your favorite!" she said.

"I know," Max agreed quietly. "And I used to love to go out—maybe once every couple of weeks—as David. When no one knew what I was doing, and when no one knew who I was. I loved it. It was fun. And I did it because it was part of the magic, it was really the whole reason for the park. But now . . . well, now I'm doing it because I have to. And there's a funny difference."

Reggie hesitated a minute. "We are going to beat this thing."

"Or go down swinging," he agreed.

Reggie smiled slowly and turned, heading for the doorway.

"Watch out for him, Reggie," Max suddenly called after her.

She stiffened, then swung around, feigning innocence. "I—I don't know what you're talking about."

"Yes, you do. I'm talking about Wes."

"What do you mean?"

"Play straight with him, that's what I'm saying."

She set a hand on her hip. "Wait a minute. Excuse me. You're my brother. Aren't you supposed to be telling him to play straight with me?"

"You have a habit of wanting things to fall into nice, neat little niches. You want men to behave as you want them to."

Reggie gasped. "What on earth are you talking about? I haven't even seen any men since—"

"Right," Max agreed. "Because you didn't want anyone close. Nowhere near close. You shut doors. I'm just warning you. You never pull a wolf by the tail, Reggie."

"There! You just said it. Go talk to your friend, the wolf!" Reggie returned.

Max smiled. "Do I need to talk to my friend, the wolf?" he queried politely, jet dark brows at an angle.

"You need to mind your own affairs, my dear sibling," she warned him. Her chin was rising. She turned to leave the room.

She heard his soft laughter following in her wake.

*   *   *

By noon she had hopped around as Dierdre Dinosaur—which was fun!—helped out in the bakery kitchen, joined a parade as a dino-riding toy soldier and started to put some things in order in the costume shop.

Once upon a time, before the Daphne misery had begun, the costume shop would never have been in such bad shape. But before the Daphne misery had come up, there had always been at least one escort for every three people playing dinosaurs, and there had always been someone in the costume shop. Now the busy players were hastily shedding their costumes and hurrying on to some other position at the park, and the costumes were being thrust into general positions on the racks and hangers, but not being put away properly.

If Daphne was all right, and if she was trying to destroy the park, she was doing a very fine job of it.

Since she had nibbled on croissants while in the bakery that morning, Reggie decided that she could definitely forgo lunch. She spent the noon hour trying to begin to set the main costume shop straight.

Each show—and there were several of them—had its own costume shop and dressing rooms for the actors. But this was the main shop, and it was where all costumes were repaired, where they were made to begin with and where the bulk of them were stored.

The main theme of the park was dinosaurs, but the costume list was extensive. There were subthemes to the park, like the saloon show where the men were men and the women were women—they rode dinosaurs instead of horses, that was all.

Then there was the hall of history—where history was altered just a bit so that dino-cars could take the park guests from the days of the tar pits right up to the space age. Part of the exhibit was done with robotronics, or mannequins programmed to speak and move realistically. But the exhibit closed with a live performance with dancers and singers, some of them dinosaurs, some of them just friends of dinosaurs. Then there was a segment of the park on peoples of the world, featuring a show with a multitude of tunes and dances from all over the globe. All these costumes were stored in the main shop, too, along with the occasional broken robotronic figure or one that was being redressed or rewigged to take on another identity.

It could be an eerie place.

Reggie had never thought so before, but today, at noon, she stood in the shop all alone.

A half-clad woman with widespread Nordic pigtails stared at her with a sunny smile from across the room. There was a Hungarian count beside her, a fellow with slicked-back dark hair and a Dracula cape. He wasn't smiling.

The artist had given him fantastic eyes. They seemed to follow Reggie.

"Oh, you stop it!" she told the figure suddenly. She had been stuffing the top half of a Dierdre costume into its proper square cubicle when she felt ripples of unease scoot up her spine. And when she turned, certain that someone was in the room with her, she had discovered that it was none other than the diabolically handsome Hungarian.

"You!" She wagged a finger at the figure. "Don't get uppity with me. I'm pretty sure you're one of my own sketches." She moved closer to the figure, then smiled at her sense of unease.

She had been the first one to sketch him. He bore a marked resemblance to Max. She turned away from the figure and started stuffing costumes into cubicles again. She glanced at her watch. She had to make certain she gave herself enough time to get to the show. She wished she could shake the feeling that she was being watched.

Think about Wes, that should do it, she told herself. Or think about Wes and Max. Be mad at the two of them!

Damn Max. Just what the hell had he been warning her about? Well, if he thought she was teasing Wes, wanting someone to practice her wiles upon, he was way off the mark.

"He won't be demanding anything he thinks I've offered because I've offered it all," she murmured softly.

I offered too much....

And where had it gotten her?

Just where she wanted to be. He was angry with her now, she knew. Because she had been pretending that things were entirely aboveboard. No, they were both adults; things were aboveboard.

I just refrained from making an announcement! she defended herself.

What had he wanted from her? she wondered.

No ghosts. He had said something about ghosts. That there was a difference between not wanting to be alone, and wanting to be with someone.

But she had. And she had wanted to be with him.

And she hadn't given a thought to anyone other than him from the moment she had come to him. She hadn't seen anyone else or thought of anyone else.

No ghost of Caleb.

Honesty. It was what he wanted.

She groaned softly, thrust a big dinosaur head into its cubicle and moved to the oak desk. She sat down in the red-upholstered swivel chair behind it. She pressed the soda can she'd brought in with her against her temple, feeling it cool her. She popped the top and drank several swallows of the bubbly liquid, then swallowed a hiccup.

She stared at the old Victorian love seat, with its two matching armchairs, that sat across from the desk. Once upon a time, employees had gathered here. They had sat around to chat when their shifts were over. It had always been a warm place.

Now, the love seat was taken up by a half-clad, pretty, blond robotronic and the back half of a dinosaur costume. Reggie didn't like the blond robotronic. She seemed to be looking at Reggie, too.

Reggie groaned and laid her head on the desk. "Between my brother and his absurd problems and pesty friends, I am losing my sanity."

She stared at the blonde again.

"I never had it, eh, is that what you're saying?" She laid her head down again. "No, that's not true. I did have it. Really, I did. Until last night."

She drummed her fingers absently on the desk. So Wes wanted honesty. What else?

What did he want from her?

Wes certainly hadn't spent the last years in a fantasy world as she had. Maybe he had stayed in love with the woman he had lost, but he had made love with other women since then. He was an accomplished lover. He knew what he wanted, and he knew how to get it. And he knew how to give. How to touch. How to kiss...

So he had had lovers. Women to ease the pain. To break the loneliness.

And now she was one of them.

She inhaled and exhaled sharply. He had seduced her. No, *she* had gone to him. She was a big girl. She had wanted him, and she'd had him.

And for the moment, she still had.

So just what would she do with him?

She didn't know. She suddenly felt numb. The coolness of the oak beneath her cheek felt wonderful. She shouldn't be thinking about Wes now. He was angry with her, but she had been playing it as honestly as she could. She had seen him, only him, in bed last night.

And when she closed her eyes, she saw him again. Saw the platinum tufts of coarse hair that splayed across his chest. Saw the bronze flesh beneath it. She could almost feel it beneath her fingers, so tense, so vital. Feel the ripple of muscle. Remember touching him. Running her fingers over his chest, down the leanness of his belly. Watching the way his hair darkened and thickened to nest the rod of his sex. See the pulse...

His flesh, his eyes. His face. The curve of a smile. Fading. Laughter replaced by tension as passion grew, as he thrust into her...

Her eyes flew open. She had always had way too vivid an imagination.

She was again drawn to the robotronic on the love seat. The mannequin seemed to be watching her.

"Thank God I have to go do that show!" she told herself aloud, pushing back in the chair to rise.

She was off to play a sleazy dance hall girl. When she'd been having such sleazy thoughts. Well, it *was* fitting.

"See you later," she told the figure on the love seat.

But as she locked the door, she didn't feel at all sleazy about the way she had been with Wes.

She felt good.

She hadn't felt so good since...

Years. She hadn't felt so good in years.

And still...

He would stay with her until this mess was solved. What then?

Did it matter?

It would.

But did it matter now?

No. He would be sleeping with her tonight. And for now, it was all she wanted. It was enough.

Several hours later, she fitted her key into the lock again.

She had enjoyed doing the show. Granted, it hadn't been as good as it had been with Wes in the audience, and she had been halfway expecting him to appear there, waiting for her. But he didn't appear, and of course the show wasn't quite as good.

But it was still good. She enjoyed working with Bob, Stevie and Alise. And when it had been over, the three had managed to get Reggie to promise that she would fill in with them until they were able to find a permanent replacement.

They all knew that might take a little while.

In return, they vowed their loyalty again. They knew Max was innocent, and they wouldn't be leaving.

As she opened the costume shop door, she felt suddenly tired. She walked in, slumped into the chair and wished she could go home.

She had promised, though. She had told Wes she would be here.

Maybe she didn't have the energy to move, anyway.

And besides, she couldn't go home to peace and quiet. Diana would be there.

With that thought in mind, Reggie groped for the phone and dialed her own number. She clenched her teeth as she heard the answering machine come on. She waited for the beep.

"Diana, this is Reggie. If you're there, please pick up. Please—"

"Reggie! Are you all right?"

Reggie frowned. "Of course, I'm all right. Why?"

"I'm talking about last night. How horrible that someone was in here! What an awful invasion."

Yes, it was, Reggie reflected. "I'm all right, really."

"That's what Max said. Thank goodness you weren't alone."

"Right," Reggie murmured.

"And that *he* stayed with you. Mr. tall, blond and handsome, that is."

Reggie hesitated, staring at the receiver. Diana spoke quickly.

"Oh, you know that I adore your brother! But if I didn't... well, Mr. Blake just has something... special! Don't you think?"

"Mmm. Special," she agreed grudgingly. Then she added quickly, "Thank you, Diana. I really appreciate you going out there today."

"Think nothing of it. I'm working on the sketches for the Christmas show. It didn't matter one whit whether I worked on them here or there."

"Still, I appreciate it. Do I have an alarm system?"

"You do. And it seems to be marvelously simple—you just have to press some numbers like a phone. And we're all pretty good at phones, eh?"

"Um, I guess," Reggie agreed.

"And it seems to be complete. There are tiny wires in the windows, and the doors are covered. I'll be able to teach you to use it in a matter of minutes."

"That sounds great."

"I hope this sounds great, too," Diana said. "Max promised to come out and take me home tonight. He said he'd get here around eight. I went ahead and ordered up some stuff to barbecue for dinner. I figured that everyone had to eat. I thought it might be nice—relaxing—to eat by the pool and maybe take a dip before or after. What do you think?"

What did she think? Panic seized her. She was going to have to sit there with her brother and Diana and Wes in a social situation. Just like a double date.

"If it's not all right, just say so," Diana told her. "I'll understand."

"No, no!" Reggie said quickly. Diana had sat over there all day long for her benefit.

Diana had also done a lot more. While everyone speculated that Max might be a murderer, Diana had valiantly stayed glued to his arm, telling the world that anyone who thought Max was a murderer had to be daft. She wasn't afraid in the least to go home alone with him at any time.

"A barbecue sounds wonderful, Diana. Especially if we can make Max do the cooking."

"I'll do the cooking if he won't, Reggie."

"That's great."

"Tall, blond and handsome will be with you?"

"Oh, yes," Reggie murmured.

"Good. Come soon."

Diana hung up. Reggie tiredly aimed the receiver in the direction of the phone. As she rested her head on the desk, she stared at the Victorian love seat in front of her and slowly started to frown.

Something was different.

She remembered the blond robotronic figure that had been there before. The hair had been short; the girl hadn't been wearing a shirt. In fact, she'd only had one arm, if Reggie remembered correctly.

The figure was different now. There was a whole bunch of blond hair, lying like a bad wig over the face.

The figure was clad in an encompassing cloak.

Actually, it wasn't a figure at all....

It was real.

It suddenly leaped to its feet, pointing her way with a black-gloved hand. "Reggie!" it exclaimed hoarsely, the voice deep and low, like that of a crypt keeper. "Your brother is a killer! And you're going to die!"

Reggie gasped, stunned. She jumped to her feet, terrified, ready to scream hysterically.

Then sanity grabbed hold of her.

There was a person in the cloak. A person trying to ruin her brother's life.

Her life.

The park.

"All right!" she snapped out, starting around the desk. But she was shaking still. "You just wait! You can talk to the police—"

She broke off, fear snaking along her spine, her breath gone, as the lights went off.

She was pitched into total blackness.

A chill laughter sounded.

"Reggie's going to die!" the harsh voice called out sharply, like one child taunting another.

"And you're going to jail!" Reggie said, trying hard for a show of bravado. The lights! She had to reach the main switch. Don't panic, turn!

No! Don't turn on a light! Wes had said not to turn on the light. Just get out, get out.

But she heard the laughter again. Horrible. Shrill.

Then she heard a whisking in the air. Instinctively, she ducked.

The phone on her desk went clattering to the floor. Something had whacked it.

She choked back a scream. She had to get out. She couldn't see her tormentor.

Her tormentor couldn't possibly see her.

"Reggie . . ."

She heard the taunting, sexless whisper. Then she thought she saw a glimmer of light. The door.

Something suddenly fell over her head. A sheet. No—a roll of dinosaur-colored fabric. She threw it off, throwing caution to the wind.

The material fell around her again.

And in the darkness, arms reached out for her. Fingers wound around her elbows.

She screamed. She cast back her head and screamed at the top of her lungs.

"Reggie!"

She was fighting to come up from some awful darkness. It was no longer the taunting voice that came to her.

The hood of material was thrown off. The lights were on.

Wes was holding her.

Wes. And Max was behind him.

"Reggie, Reggie! What in God's name—" Max began.

Wes was staring at her, golden eyes searing questioningly into hers.

And at that moment, she didn't care that Max was there.

And she didn't care in the very least what the future might bring.

She lay her head against Wes's chest, her fingers falling lightly against him.

"Oh, Wes!"

He lifted her, cradling her against him. And he walked her out of the darkness of the costume shop and into the light beyond.

Chapter 9

The park, thankfully, was empty. Darkness was falling. Far away, down the main thoroughfare, Reggie could see that one of the sweepers, a tall man in cleaning crew whites, was sweeping. There were other cleanup people around, somewhere. And there were security guards, walking their rounds.

But no one was near enough to see how upset Reggie had been.

How frightened.

It took her several minutes to begin to make sense.

She was seated on one of the little wooden dino-chairs at Dierdre's Dino-mite Burgers and Dogs. Wes had sat her there when he had carried her out, and for several long minutes he had remained on his knees before her, holding her hands, telling her she was all right.

As she had calmed herself, she had drawn back her hands guiltily and looked around. She was alone, really truly alone out here, except for her brother and Wes.

And now they were staring at her as she tried to explain what had happened. Max was next to her. Wes was standing, his arms crossed over his chest, his left foot resting on the rung of one of the chairs.

The crew who sold burgers and dogs were all gone. A pleasant, spicy scent remained around the area, and Reggie was very glad of it. The scent was something that seemed to drag her back to normal. Once she got over being scared, she promised herself, she was going to be hungry.

"The robotronic talked?" Max said.

"Yes. It stood up and it talked," Reggie said numbly. Wes had grown quiet. She felt a stiffness about him, a certain withdrawal.

It was because she had jerked her hands away, she knew. She hadn't meant to do it. She just wasn't sure she had the nerve to face up to a relationship right now.

"Reggie," Max said, glancing from Wes to her. He was irritatingly patient. "Robotronics are supposed to talk," he reminded her.

She stared at him blankly. "What?"

"Robotronics are created to talk, Reggie. They're supposed to be very real—"

"Max!" She clenched her fingers into fists and leaped to her feet. "It wasn't a robotronic!"

"Reggie, you just told me that there had been a blond robotronic on the love seat—"

"You weren't listening to me!" She stared from her brother to Wes. He stared back, lifting his hands in a vague motion.

"It is what you said," Wes told her dryly.

"Oh, you know what I mean! It was supposed to have been a robotronic. You weren't paying any attention to me, either of you!" Reggie said angrily.

"Oh, I was paying attention," Wes said lightly.

"She's just been working too many hours," Max murmured.

"With no sleep," Wes agreed.

She wanted to knock their heads together. Instead she touched Max on the shoulder.

"I'm here, remember?" she said accusingly. "I am not overtired, and I am not—"

"He's the one who said that you were overtired," Max pointed out, a finger wagging at Wes. "And just exactly why is she so tired?" he asked suddenly.

"You'll have to ask Reggie about that," Wes said flatly. He was staring at her. Hard.

She swallowed. "Would you two stop! Whoever was in there is getting away."

There was a silence. Then Wes sighed softly, staring at her again. "Reggie, there was no one in there. You were all alone."

"But I wasn't! I'm telling you—"

"Yes," Wes interrupted, standing, shoving his hands into his pockets. "There's a blond robotronic figure on the love seat, just like you said. There's no one else in there."

"How do you know? It was dark. Someone was attacking me. I fought back. I fought someone."

"Reggie, you were trying to thrash me," Wes told her.

She gritted her teeth, praying for patience. "Yes, I was with you!" she snapped. "So you certainly weren't going through the costume shop, looking for anyone else!"

"I looked," Max said. "As soon as Wes brought you out here, I went in and looked."

"What?" Dumbfounded, she stared at her brother.

"Reggie, I looked. Wes had you, and I did the looking. I got the lights on as fast as possible, and I searched around. There was no one in there."

"Someone was!" she insisted furiously.

"There's only the one main door," Max said. "There in the hallway."

"Right—and then there are the two dressing rooms!" she reminded him.

"No one came into the hallway, Reggie. We would see anyone who did," Wes told her.

He could speak for himself, she thought. During the immediate moments when he brought her out of the shop, he wouldn't have seen a damn thing.

She stared furiously at Wes. "What is the matter with both of you? I'm telling you, there was someone in there with me. How can you doubt me? Max, did you really look? Or did you just assume I was having some hysterical fit of exhaustion?" she asked angrily.

"Reggie, I know the shop. I looked," he returned. "But we can call security and have them go through the place, too."

"I imagine it would be too late now," Wes said. "If someone was there—"

"Someone was there!" Reggie insisted. "Maybe whoever it was is gone now, but I didn't imagine it."

Wes stared at her. His arms were still crossed over his chest, his face hard. There was no humor to the curl of his lip. "Are you sure, Reggie? The lights didn't just go out and frighten you?"

"I was tangled in a cloak—"

"You might have done that yourself."

"Yes, I might have. But I didn't. And if you don't want to believe me—"

"I do believe you," he told her. Despite everything, she felt her heart skip a little beat.

"What was this thing saying to you?" Wes asked her.

She swallowed hard, then stared at her brother. "It was saying that you were a murderer. And that—"

Max's eyes narrowed sharply. "And what else?"

"And that I was going to die."

Max stared at her. Something veiled seemed to fall over her brother's eyes.

"Don't you dare look at me like that!" she charged him. "None of this is my imagination! And I have never lost faith in you! How can you lose it in me so easily?"

"Hey!" Wes interrupted quietly, "let's slow down here, huh? If someone is out to destroy the park, the best way to do it would be to put the two of you at odds, right?"

Reggie exhaled slowly. She saw Max blink, and that defensive barrier of his was gone. "All right. Let's slow down and start over. Max, Wes, I'm neither hysterically tired nor just plain crazy. When I went into the costume shop after the show, I didn't pay any attention to the love seat. I called Diana to see about my house. Then, when I hung up, I realized that it wasn't the same robotronic sitting there. Then I realized that it wasn't a robotronic at all. Max, Wes, damn you both! Someone came in there purposely to goad me or to really hurt me—I'm not sure which! And that same someone figured out some way to disappear!''

"I'll take a walk through," Wes said lightly. "It has to be too late to catch anyone up to tricks, but maybe there will be something in there to find."

He walked through the main door and disappeared. Max clasped Reggie's hand lightly. "Sorry," he said softly. His lashes were low over his cheeks. "Damn it, Reggie, don't you see? I want you to be hysterical. I'm getting scared to death that you are going to get hurt for some sort of transgression on my part!"

"I'm—I'm not going to get hurt," Reggie said quickly. "I'm all right, really." But she hadn't been, she thought. She had been terrified.

That's because she hadn't been ready for what had happened. But no one would be able to play such a trick on her again. She would never think, in her wildest imagination, that an oversize, electronic mannequin could come to life—even for a fraction of a second!

Next time she'd get hold of the human-in-costume—and she'd do so quickly!

Max started to say something, but Wes was on his way to them. He had something in his hands.

A pair of gloves. Long dark gloves.

He handed them to Reggie. "These were stuffed into a small compartment in the rear. One was dangling." He looked at Max. "And there is another way out of the shop."

Max frowned.

"The fire exit," Wes said.

"But the alarm would have sounded."

"Not when the alarm was turned off," Wes said.

"Turned off!" Max exclaimed. He looked at Reggie.

"I didn't do it!" She let out a soft expletive. "I swear to you both, someone was in there."

"Well, then, maybe we need to call Wiler again," Max said wearily, rubbing his temple between his thumb and forefinger.

"There's nothing we can do here," Wes said, his hands on his hips. He shook his head. "They can dust for prints, but they'll come up with dozens of them. We'll call Wiler. But let's get out of here first."

"Let's." For the first time in her life, Reggie really wanted to leave the park.

She almost hated dinosaurs.

No! she told herself. She couldn't stop loving the dinosaurs because they had come first. They had started the dream. The park, the buildings, the food concessions, the rides, the shows, they had all come after.

The dinosaurs had created the magic.

And she refused to lose it.

Reggie sluiced cleanly through the water, swimming hard and with an energy that was startling after the length of her day.

But the water felt good. It was deliciously cool. And when she slowed at last, floating on her back and barely paddling to keep that way, she stared at the moon high above then closed her eyes for a moment appreciating the sensations of the water. She closed her eyes again.

It was beautiful out here. It was the kind of balmy night that was just perfect. There was the slightest breeze, but not enough to make the air cold. The moon was vivid against the velvet darkness of the sky. It was a full moon. Vibrantly full.

The kind of full moon beneath which movie vampires stalked their prey. Mmm, yes. The kind of full moon that turned gentle men like Lon Chaney, Jr., into furious and furry werewolves.

The kind of moon . . .

That turned robotronics into living creatures?

She felt water move by her, then she shivered, startled by the ripple of pleasure that streaked through her as masculine hands touched her, moving over the bare flesh at her midriff. She opened her eyes, not at all alarmed despite the recent ghoulish twist in her thoughts.

Wes was beside her.

She straightened, treading water, meeting his gaze. It was not easy being here like this, even though the night was going very nicely. They'd all talked little on the drive out to her house. But once they'd arrived, Diana had somehow managed to break the tension that had been forming, demanding to know what had happened. Reggie had been extremely grateful for her instant faith. They'd called Wiler, who had said he'd be in to see her in the morning. When Reggie had talked briefly with Wiler, she had been surprised to discover that Wes had spent the majority of the day at the police station. But with everyone's concentration being on her and what had happened in the costume shop, she'd had no chance to question Wes. And when she had gotten off the phone, Diana had assured them that she had the food well under control, that the three of them should take a swim, the water was beautiful. And Reggie, wanting nothing to do with her brother or Wes at the moment, had begun to swim laps, and the laps had slowly taken the tension from her.

And now, looking at Wes, she found herself appreciating some very basic things about him. She loved the bronzed coloring of his shoulders. She loved the way he was built, strong, lean and taut, with muscles that rippled subtly rather than bulged, long, strong thighs and lean hips, an altogether very attractive package. Now, his fingers moving lightly against her midriff, left bare by what she had once thought to be a fairly decent bikini, she could almost forget that they weren't alone, that her brother—elder by those five minutes—was watching her with concerned interest.

She met Wes's gaze, the gold of his eyes enhanced by the reflection of the water. Then, despite herself, she found herself glancing toward the barbecue and her brother and Diana. It was a mistake. She caught the mocking curl of Wes's lip. "I was sent," he told her. "The food is just about ready."

"Oh," she murmured awkwardly.

"I don't play games, Reggie," he warned her.

"I don't know what you're talking about."

"I think you do."

She shrugged. "Whatever—"

"With Max. With me. You can't keep pretending that nothing has happened."

"For your information, Mr. Blake, Max warned me to be careful with you."

He smiled suddenly. "And for your information, Miss Delaney, Max warned me about you, too."

"Oh!" she exclaimed. Then she frowned. "Why?"

"I'm not sure."

"Well, he is my brother. He should be defending my honor."

"Maybe. Or maybe he was warning me that you liked to use men."

"Me!" Reggie flared. Damn! She was blushing again. "I've barely gone so far as to have dinner—"

"Maybe that's the point," he said softly. She was startled at the heat in his eyes as they focused pointedly on her. "Tell me something."

"What?"

"Why didn't you marry him?"

"What?" she repeated. She had heard him. She just wasn't ready with an answer. Where had he come up with a question like that?

"Why didn't you ever marry Caleb?"

There was water between them. A foot of it, at least. Gallons of it, maybe. Yet it seemed that she could feel the heat of him. And the strength of him. Something almost overwhelming. Something that nearly choked her. "It's none of your business!" she rasped out. Pain seemed to come rushing to her. The pain of losing him.

The pain of what she might have given, what she had held back. Pain she had never meant to inflict.

Something dark flickered across his hazel gaze as he studied her intently. Something tightened around his mouth and he asked, "Does being Miss Delaney mean that much to you?"

"What?" She gasped, amazed. Then her temper soared. She was furious that he would believe such a thing of her so simply.

"Damn it, Reggie, you're hearing me quite well, I know it."

"Oh, yes, I heard you! That the Delaney name was worth more to me than a relationship."

"It is a well-known name," he said. He didn't back down, she thought. Ever.

"You've no right to accuse me—"

"I'm not accusing. I'm asking."

"Like I said before, it's none of your business. Think what you want!"

She turned, and with a powerful stroke started to swim away. He caught her arm, pulling her against him in the water. For a moment, their physical contact was so acute that she could scarcely breathe. But the tension in his grip, the anger in his eyes, made her fight for a defensive stance with him, and she steeled herself against him.

"It is my business," he stated flatly.

"Why?"

"Because I'm sleeping with you now. I want to know."

Tears were suddenly stinging her eyes. "Well, I don't want to tell you."

"Reggie—"

"Maybe he never asked me."

"But he did. Max told me that he did."

"Well, then, go back and ask Max whatever else you want to know, too!"

"Damn you, Reggie, you're the one I'm sleeping with!"

"Well, you don't have to continue to do so."

His fingers curled around her arm so tightly that she nearly cried out. She could feel the tremendous power of his legs as he treaded water, keeping them both afloat. For a moment she nearly cowered. Just how well did she know him? He was so angry he might have lashed out and struck her.

No, she thought. She knew him well enough. He would never strike her.

He pulled her close. There was no distance at all between them in the water. She felt the powerful thrust of his legs. Felt the heat of his flesh brushing hers. She thought perhaps he was going to wind his arms around her. Lock her into an endless, passionate embrace that would bring them both sinking to the bottom, heedless of whether they could breathe or not. And she'd have no choice but to say something to Max because Wes would be halfway making love to her right there.

She trembled, her lips parting, for his were moving closer and closer to hers. Longing and desire flashed through her, and she was amazed at the wanton heat that filled her when other people—her brother among them!—were so close.

But he wasn't going to kiss her. Not at the moment. She could feel both of them, as if they would combust. And she could feel his anger, fierce, dark, compelling.

But then he thrust her away from him.

"Fine, Miss Delaney," he said softly. "I don't force any woman," he added bluntly.

Then suddenly she was adrift and on her own.

She started to sink beneath the water. She quickly kicked against it and swam to the steps that would take her to dry land.

She was shaking. Shaking so badly that she wasn't sure she could climb the steps.

"Reggie! Come on!" Diana urged.

She found the step. Suddenly she realized that Wes was back, offering a hand to her. Her cheeks were flaming. She hated him at that moment.

He was asking too much of her. Far too much. And she really didn't know what he was offering in return.

"Give me your hand. You don't seem to be able to make it out."

"I can make it out," she assured him quickly. "I can make it without you in any way."

"Give me your hand!"

She told him in explicit terms just what he could do with himself.

He arched a brow, then took her by the wrist, whether she had planned to offer her hand to him or not. And when he had lifted her from the water he drew her close once again, his words offered for her ears alone. "Maybe I touched a nerve. A real nerve. If so, I'm sorry. But if you do want me to sleep with you again, Miss Delaney, you had best ask. And nicely."

"What nerve—" she began furiously, shaking again, and wishing that the searing stare from his hazel eyes wasn't making her feel hot inside despite the force of the breeze.

She didn't get any further.

"Towel, Reggie!" Max called. He threw her a huge bath towel. Wes caught it. And wrapped it around her.

It was one they sold at the park. There was a huge, friendly-looking Dierdre Dinosaur on the towel.

I can't escape! she thought desperately. There were dinosaurs everywhere in her life.

Hadn't she made it that way herself? she wondered. Wes was staring at her still. His lip curled into a taunting grin, as if he was reading her mind.

Yes, her life had been dinosaurs.

But she had needed the dinosaurs!

And now...

Despite her harsh words, she was afraid she was beginning to need something else. Someone else.

Wes.

Chapter 10

She would have spoken then, but he wrapped the towel around her, then walked away. She paused for a moment, breathing deeply.

She walked around from the ladder to the barbecue and picnic table, which were elevated on a brick dais at the left side of the pool. Farther back, there was a screened-in free-standing patio. She'd had it made to avoid the bugs that sometimes came heavily in the summer. She hadn't wanted the pool screened in, though, even if it did make the maintenance a little tougher and even if there were bugs in summer. She had always loved to be in the water, looking up at the sky.

And tonight, they hadn't attracted more than a daring fly or two. By the time Reggie walked to the picnic table, Diana had seen to it that all the food was arranged and covered. She'd done a nice job with dinner. There were ribs and chicken, her special baked beans, corn on the cob and a sweet and sour salad. She and Max had eschewed the table to take seats on one of the lounges. Max, with a chicken leg in his fingers, was sitting at the rear of it, and Diana was comfortably leaned against him. Diana popped a cucumber into his mouth, asking if he liked the dressing.

It was nice. It seemed especially domestic, and close, something warm between them. Reggie felt a peculiar fire streak through her, and she was aware, even before she glanced at him, that Wes was watching her, and watching her reaction to the other couple. Just what the hell does Wes want out of me? she wondered irritably.

He hadn't made his plate of food yet—he was waiting for her to do so. But maybe she was moving too slowly. He stepped beside her, piled his plate high, praising Diana for the meal, then took a seat on another of the pool chairs.

"Want a beer, Wes?" Max asked.

"Yeah, thanks."

"Reggie, they're in the cooler there," Diana said. "Grab one for Wes, will you?"

She gritted her teeth. It was her house. Mmm. And she should be hospitable. Especially because Max and Diana would leave. And then she would be left alone with Wes.

Wes, whom she had angered. And then she had told him he could go...

And she really didn't want him to walk away on her. To leave her.

He wouldn't leave her. He had some kind of code of honor that wouldn't let him do that. He was a cavalier, she reminded herself.

But she didn't want him to just stay. She wanted him to hold her again.

To sleep with her, to make love to her.

She just didn't want him to ask questions. And she hated it that he seemed to think the worst of her with no questions asked.

Silently, she handed him a beer. Their fingers brushed. Warmth came sweeping through her. She wanted to sit in front of him, the way Diana was sitting in front of Max. She felt his gaze.

She couldn't meet his eyes.

She decided to have a beer herself. She popped the top and took a seat at the picnic table, her Dierdre Dinosaur towel wrapped around her waist.

"Tell me what happened again, Reggie," Diana said suddenly, staring thoughtfully at her ear of corn.

Reggie sighed. She'd explained it so many times. "The robotronic on the love seat wasn't a robotronic at all. I hung up from talking to you and the figure jumped up and pointed at me and told me that Max was a murderer and that I was going to die."

"And last night, there was someone in your house," Diana added.

"It's as if someone was out to get Regina instead of Max," Wes said.

"Maybe you should go somewhere safe," Max said suddenly. "Maybe somebody *is* out to hurt you."

"I can't go anywhere!" Reggie said. "I have to stay—I'm filling in for half a dozen employees, remember? Besides, it's not my ex-wife who is missing."

"Thank goodness!" Diana said lightly. "That definitely would have set the whole affair in a very strange light!"

Even Reggie smiled.

"Someone is trying to get to Max through Reggie, I think," Wes said after a moment. "Attack Reggie often enough, and her faith in Max begins to falter."

Reggie shook her head. "But that would never happen."

Max sat up, his arms lightly around Diana. Watching the couple, Reggie stiffened miserably.

I want to be held like that! she thought. But she was busy destroying what she had nearly managed to hold.

"Didn't you wonder, even for a moment, when this—thing suggested that I was a murderer?" Max asked her.

Reggie frowned. "Of course not."

"But you were frightened, right?" Wes said.

Reggie started to deny it. Those damned eyes of his. She couldn't do so. "Yes. I suppose I was frightened." She was beginning to feel cornered by him, and was determined to turn the tables. "What were you doing at the police station all day?"

He waved a hand, the one with his beer in it, in a vague motion. "Things."

"Like?"

"Checking into people."

"Like who?"

"Stockholders. People associated with the park. People in your pasts."

"And have you found anything?"

"Answers are rarely found in a day," he told her. Then he leaned forward, watching her. "Unless..."

"Unless what?"

"What did you discover today?"

"I don't know what you mean."

"Think. Tell me about this figure. Tall? Thin? Heavy? Male or female?"

Reggie frowned. She hadn't thought about the figure at all, not in those terms. She tried to think. "Medium, I think. No taller than I am."

"A woman?" Diana asked. "What about the voice?"

Reggie shook her head. "I couldn't tell. I really couldn't tell. It was disguised. Hoarse. And I was so frightened...."

"But still, the height would suggest a woman, right?" Wes said.

"Right," Reggie agreed reluctantly. Then she stared at him accusingly. "If she was *real*, of course. If I didn't *imagine* her."

"Max and I have both said that we don't think you imagined her, Reggie," Wes said.

Yes, they had. But they certainly hadn't believed her at first.

"I think it's only a matter of time before this person—or these *persons*—trip themselves up," Diana said determinedly.

Reggie hoped so. She noticed that Wes was staring at Diana, reflecting on her words, intrigued. But Diana seemed to be the eternal optimist that night. "More chicken anyone? Ribs? How about some coffee, decaf or tea?"

"I'll make the coffee," Reggie said, standing up. "You did everything else."

"I didn't mind," Diana said. "And you specifically said that you didn't want to do the cooking tonight."

"I was tired," Reggie said hastily. "But really, I feel the need to move at the moment. I'll put coffee on and pick up a few things here. You relax for a few minutes. With Max." She had added the last words in a rush, and then she wondered why she had done so. She wasn't implying that Wes should help her, or that he should leave Max and Diana alone. It was just that the two of them looked so comfortable together, and she really did appreciate all that Diana was doing. Especially the way that she was standing by Max.

"If you want some help—" Diana said.

She shook her head. "I'm fine. I'll mix it up, half decaf and half one of the special blends."

"There are éclairs in the refrigerator," Diana told her.

Reggie had collected a few of the plates. She nodded. "You just whipped those up this afternoon, right?"

Diana smiled. "You had the ingredients," she said apologetically.

"They sound great."

Reggie hurried toward the house, wondering why she had commented on Diana's cooking skills. It had to be because she was just a little bit jealous of the other woman.

Somehow, Diana had made Reggie seem so undomestic tonight. Reggie didn't know why it mattered. She wasn't a great cook or housekeeper. That was why she had Mrs. Martin. She was too busy.

And Diana wasn't that great anyway! she reminded herself. But it bothered her tonight.

Maybe it was because of Wes's assessment of why she hadn't married Caleb. He had certainly hit upon something vulnerable within her.

Inside the house she threw away the paper plates she had picked up and tossed the flatware into the sink. She delved into the freezer for the coffee, deciding to mix some French vanilla beans with a decaffeinated Columbian blend. She had pulled out the pot and the water and was grinding the beans when the back door opened and Wes walked in, tossing more plates into the trash and coming over to stand by the counter, watching her. She tensed instantly. She looked quickly from him to the grinder, very aware of how he looked in a pair of Max's cutoffs, easy and comfortable, torso and arms muscled and bronzed.

She started to shake the beans into the coffee filter and was spilling more than she was getting in. She felt him behind her, gently but firmly taking the grinder from her hands. He completed the task with no further loss of fresh ground coffee. She stood silently watching him, still angry at what he had said but not terribly pleased with her behavior toward him.

"Don't forget," he said lightly, "that you're going to have to apologize very nicely if you want me to bring you to soaring heights of ecstasy again."

"You're one egotistical creature," she retorted, then wished she had kept quiet.

His thumb was on her chin, lifting her head. "It wasn't the heights of ecstasy?"

She was turning flame red. Worse, her knees were growing very weak. "There are things that I can't answer now. They hurt."

"So it was just a little slice of heaven?" he murmured. She looked into his eyes. The warmth was there. The fire. He might have been angry. But he wasn't holding any of it against her.

"And you are ungodly good-looking," she agreed in a whisper.

He smiled. "I'm not so egotistical. Honest. I'm like an artist. Look at the canvas you gave me to work on!"

She could scarcely breathe. She felt like falling into his arms right then and there. She managed not to do so. "I am sorry," she said quickly.

He arched a brow at her, but his smile was still in place. He released her, turned and plugged the coffeepot in, then turned to her, his hands on his hips. "Like I said, I'm sorry, too, Reggie. But if there's something here, then quit acting as if there isn't," he told her.

"I don't know—"

"You do know," he said, and walked out.

When he left her, she knew that she desperately wanted there to be something. Something very special. She stared at the closed door. "Yes, you fool!" she whispered after him. "I'll start to think that there is something, I'll get involved, and you'll just—"

Go away.

She clenched her teeth, amazed at the moisture in her eyes. She didn't even know what she wanted! Just a few more nights of solace, a touch in the dark.

More.

"Damn him!" she whispered. Then she reached into the refrigerator for the éclairs. They were already arranged on a flowered paper platter. Reggie picked them up, found some more paper plates and napkins and started out with them.

She almost crashed into Wes. He was coming in with the barbecue utensils. He walked around her silently, and she could hear him placing the things in the sink, then reaching into her cupboard for cups.

She went out to the picnic table with the éclairs. Diana and Max were talking softly, looking at the sky. Max leaned back in the lounge, his arm lightly around her. They were an attractive couple. Max, so dark and handsome. Diana with her trim figure, short blond hair and pretty, aristocratic features and velvet brown eyes.

Loyal to the core. Diana was even wearing a one-piece Dierdre Dinosaur bathing suit.

"Let me get up and help you with that stuff," Diana began.

Reggie waved a hand in the air. "Sit tight. You look very comfortable. And Wes is helping."

Wes *was* helping. He was coming out with the brewed coffee and cups on a tray. Reggie started toward the house with the barbecue sauce, salt, pepper and salad bowl balanced in her arms.

"Grab milk and sugar," he told her. She nodded.

When she came out with them, he was seated at the picnic table, his legs straddled over the bench. She set the cream and sugar on the tray, then hesitated briefly before sitting beside him.

Close beside him.

She felt his eyes on her as she poured coffee into four cups. Diana roused herself to get a cup, black with sugar, for herself, and one with cream, sugarless, for Max. Wes helped himself to a cup, his fingers idly moving over the rim. Reggie lifted a cup for herself, tasted the coffee and stared at Wes's chest.

She wanted to lean against it. Just to lean against him and look at the moon, feel the breeze and his arms around her.

They had made love so passionately, so intimately. But now, something that was so natural and warm seemed far too assuming for her to do.

But she was still staring at his chest. She felt his eyes on hers, and she lifted her gaze to him. And, as if he had read her thoughts, he reached out an arm. His hand came around her middle, fingers splayed over her midriff, and he pulled her against him. Her heart missed a beat. She eased back, feeling his chin on the top of her head. She closed her eyes, amazed at the sense of security and comfort that filled her.

This was good.

And she didn't mind that Max was looking; she didn't care that anyone saw.

"Reggie, you do make the best coffee in the world," Diana told her.

Reggie smiled. At least she could make coffee.

"Thanks," she told Diana.

"Want to hit the Jacuzzi for a few minutes?" Diana asked Max. "Then we should really go. It's getting late, and you all have long days ahead of you."

The two of them were up, heading for the Jacuzzi that waterfalled into the main body of the pool from the shallow end.

Reggie didn't speak. She sipped more coffee, then felt Wes's fingers lightly moving down her cheek.

"You all right?"

She nodded, nuzzling the back of her head against his chest.

"Wes?"

"Hmm?"

"I really do want you to sleep with me again."

He was quiet for a second. She heard him swallow a sip of his coffee.

Then his whisper touched her ear. Sexy. Provocative.

"I wasn't about to miss another night beside you. No matter what you said."

"You would have come to me if I hadn't groveled?"

"I don't think you've exactly groveled."

"That's a relief."

His face, with a hint of five o'clock shadow, nuzzled hers. "I would have come for you. Words or no words, I would have had you back in my arms. Beneath me. I would have loved you, tasted you...."

Tremors swept through her. Exotic, exciting. "Please!" she whispered.

"You're right. I'm not making myself very comfortable. And even though I want Max to know about us, I really didn't mean for it to be a complete show and tell!"

She smiled, her hand resting over his where it lay against her midriff.

"I think Max is watching."

"Is he?"

"Yes."

"Then I'm getting better, don't you think?"

"Yes."

"He'll be warning us both about each other again tomorrow," Reggie said.

"That will be fine," Wes told her. He leaned closer, his whisper warm and stirring against her ear. "Just so long as he goes home pretty soon tonight."

Reggie laughed softly. The moon was beautiful, high above her. The breeze was beautiful, gentle and cool.

And his touch . . .

Was warm, comforting and exciting. Intimate. With so very much promise.

In a way, she didn't want to stir. She wanted the moment to last for a long, long time. She closed her eyes.

But Max and Diana came back. Yet even with her brother by the table, Reggie didn't move. She opened her eyes and felt his gaze upon her, then realized that he was concealing a smile.

Let him.

"We're going to go," he told Wes.

"I hate to leave you with this mess," Diana said. "You should really get some sleep."

"I am going to get some sleep. Mrs. Martin comes every day," Reggie said. "She'll be glad to have a little more to do."

Wes was behind her, his hands on her hips, while they stood in the doorway and politely waved goodbye.

She felt his lips just above her nape, brushing her flesh. Tiny bursts of warm, liquid desire began to dance their way down her spine and take root somewhere in the center of her being, then stretch out the length of her thighs and between.

"I think your brother knows we're sleeping together."

"Yes."

"And that's all right?"

"It's fine," she whispered. It was all right. It even seemed to be all right with Max. He had been the one telling her to get a life.

Wes lifted the damp length of her hair. His lips brushed her earlobe. Nibbled there.

"Damn!" he whispered. "But you do taste delicious." Then she was swinging around in his arms. "But you do need sleep," he told her gravely. His hazel eyes burned a slow-fused fire that had very little to do with rest.

She nodded solemnly in return. "But I do sleep so much better after a little exercise."

"Oh?" He arched a brow. "How do you sleep after a lot of it?"

She grinned broadly. "Just like a baby."

He swept her up into his arms. "Lots of exercise coming right up," he said huskily.

To seal the promise, he set his lips, hungry, hot on hers.

And so fused, he started up the stairs with her.

Her days were long.

Her nights were growing even longer.

He had her up the stairs quickly. So quickly. His words at the picnic table had left them both aching. She landed a bit heavily on the bed, and he was beside her. He released the hook on her bikini top and tossed the damp fabric aside, as if it had been an awful nuisance. Then his fingers were on her hips, peeling away the bikini bottom.

He stood, dropping his damp trunks. The air was cool. Her naked flesh felt very vulnerable.

And his... looked very powerful. Exciting. Hard and aroused.

Reggie reached out her arms to him, wanting to hold him, wanting to have him.

But he didn't come to her. Not right away. To her surprise, he caught her by her ankles and pulled her down to him. And his hot searing kiss landed against her midriff, and moved lower and lower.

She called his name, stunned, excited. She couldn't want him more than she did.

Yes... she could.

She was nearly sobbing, trembling, writhing, volcanic, when he rose over her at last. And when he entered her. And when she met his eyes.

And when they began to move.

And it was, indeed, a soaring height of ecstasy that they reached, one that came quickly, for they had both come to such a point of hunger. They reached a climax nearly simultaneously, shuddering, shivering, drifting downward together, damp, deliciously sated.

And a moment later, as the air cooled her feverish flesh, Reggie curled against him, holding him tight. His hand was around her. It was a wonderful feeling. One of being cherished.

He could make her so angry.

That didn't matter.

She was falling in love.

She smiled. It was a nice feeling.

Perhaps he didn't love her. Perhaps he demanded a lot from a woman even if his relationship with her remained a casual one.

It didn't matter, she thought sleepily. It felt too good to have him here. To sleep with her face against his chest. To feel the absolute comfort of his arm around her. To be naked here with him, to see the rugged texture of his fingers where his hand lay over her.

Yes...

It had been a long, long time since she had known so much. It had been a long, long time since she had known these sensations.

But it was true, she was falling in love. And she was falling in love because he was an extraordinary person.

And sometimes, to fall in love meant taking chances.

He was nearly asleep, she thought. She curled his fingers in her own and brought them to her lips, just teasing his knuckles with her lips.

"Wes?"

"Hmm?"

She breathed deeply. The hurt was still there, a pain that ran very, very deep.

"I didn't marry Caleb because my family doctor told me years ago he seriously doubted my ability to have children. And Caleb kept saying that he didn't care."

He stiffened. He had been drowsing. He was wide awake now.

"You didn't believe Caleb? He probably meant it."

She shook her head. She was glad he couldn't see her face. Tears were stinging her eyes. "No. Children are wonderful. And a man like Caleb should have had children. His own children. Children are the most important thing."

He pushed up from the bed, looking down at her. "Reggie, the world is already filled with children who need parents," he said.

"So people say. But adoption is hard. People sit there and wait and wait on lists. I couldn't be sure Caleb really wanted to do that. I wanted to—to be sure. And so—I waited."

"And he died," Wes murmured softly.

"Yes. And he died."

Wes came down beside her, wrapping his arms around her once again.

"You're wrong, Reggie."

"About what?"

"Children aren't the most important thing," he told her. His lips moved against her temple. Soft, gentle. He spoke again.

"Love is. Love is always the most important thing."

Chapter 11

In the days that followed, the tension seemed to subside a little bit.

Nothing happened. Reggie's house was left alone,
and there were no wild occurrences at the park.

Reggie settled into a startling domesticity.

She was still busy, with days that lasted well over
twelve hours.

But she was in love, and the feeling was wonderful.
It gave her energy where she might have had none left.

Wes seemed to have a wonderful instinct about her.
He disappeared on his own during the day, but he
never let her go home alone. Once, he and Max both
appeared beside her as dinosaurs, playing with the
children for the opening of the park. They were waiting for her outside the Dino Gals changing room,
ready to take her to brunch in the park. And one night
when he brought her home she was certain that a warm

bath and a glass of wine would ease her tension and give her a new life for the evening. But after the warm bath he massaged her shoulders and she fell sound asleep and when he carried her up to bed, she was dead weight rather than a temptress. But in the morning she awoke to find him nibbling her ear, and she was instantly, searingly as awake and alive as anyone could possibly want her to be. And laying against his chest for the few idle moments that they had remaining, she talked about the accident, how Caleb had been hit, how he didn't die right away, how he had gone into a coma, and how she had sat by his bedside every day for months until they had told her that his brain was dead and that they should take him off the machines. She had never talked about it. To anyone. Max had been with her most of the time, and she hadn't needed to talk to him. But she had never forgotten any of it, nor Caleb. Nor how it had felt to know that she was holding his hand in life for the last time, or to believe in her heart until the very end that what was irreversible could be reversed.

Wes didn't say much. Nothing could make something like what had happened to Caleb be all right—it never would. You just learned to live around it, Wes told her. And you didn't try to forget, because you couldn't forget. You just remembered everything that had been before. She did need to let the pictures of the end fade, and remember the days when they had laughed together, remember the Caleb who had been young and confident, who had loved her.

Later on that night she'd learned why he could speak so knowledgeably about forgetting the past. His ten-year marriage to Shelley had ended painfully, with the two of them fighting the cancer that had seized her.

"She must have been really wonderful," Reggie told him. "Max was a little bit in love with her."

Wes smiled. "Yeah, everyone was. She was beautiful, to the very end. The chemotherapy had stolen her hair, but nothing could touch her face, or her smile."

Reggie lay against him with nothing more to say. They were not divided by any of their memories. The memories were good. And Reggie told him that she was grateful for him, no matter what happened in the future, because she hadn't been able to go out with—

"Become intimate with?" he interrupted with humor.

Anyone since Caleb. She had put her nose in the air; Wes had pulled her close. People handled things in different ways. She had closed herself into a shell. Wes had looked for anything to ease the pain.

A week passed. Wes was still careful. He didn't want her to be alone. Usually, Max was with her, or Wes was with her, and sometimes she and Diana just stuck together like glue. Time was going by quickly enough, so it seemed, but nothing had been cleared up. Daphne remained missing. Wiler didn't say so, but when he passed by the house late one night to check with her, Reggie was certain that he was convinced Daphne was dead.

Her body hadn't appeared as yet.

"Well, if she is dead," Reggie told Wiler, "my brother didn't do it. Someone else did. The someone running around trying to scare me to death in the costume shop."

''What if that someone was your brother?'' Wiler said softly.

''He was with Wes!'' she exclaimed.

Wes was looking at her. He didn't say anything until Wiler left, but then she pushed him, certain that he was hiding something from her. Eventually he admitted that he and Max hadn't been together, not until they had run into one another at the costume shop.

''So you weren't together. What does that mean?'' she asked. But she knew what it meant.

''It doesn't mean anything, and that's why I didn't tell Wiler.''

Wiler would think it meant something.

He would think it meant Max might have been dressing up and trying to scare her.

If it could have been Max . . .

Then it could have been Wes, just as well.

She shivered. Wiler would surely think that the people pretending to protect her were the very ones who were threatening her.

No. Wes had been with her the night someone had been in the house.

But Wes was convinced that there had to be more than one person involved in this. He was spending day after day at the police department, tediously going through records and using his military contacts to expedite some of his searches. Or so he was telling her.

Max was innocent; Wes was innocent.

Almost a week to the day after she had been frightened by the curious robotronic figure turned live, Reggie was at the saloon show. She had stopped to talk to a number of the guests after the show, then Bob had stopped her, asking how Max was hanging in and promising his loyalty again. By the time she went in to change, Alise had gone home for the night. And when she had hung up her red dress and black fishnet stockings, it was well past seven. She came through the main theater and started out through the audience doors.

To her surprise, she found them locked. They were never locked until the cleanup crew came through, but they wouldn't be here until eight—until the guests would most certainly be gone.

"What in the world . . . ?" she murmured.

Then it settled over her. The awful feeling of being alone. And of being watched.

And of waiting for something to happen to her. Something evil.

She heard a series of loud clicking sounds.

It was the stage lights, all of them being turned off.

The overhead lights, made to look like gasoliers from the 1800s, began fading.

The light that remained was gray and misty. Fear raced along Reggie's spine. It seized her and froze her. She fought for sanity. She told herself that it was just someone trying to scare her. Someone trying to ruin the park. She would not be afraid.

But she was.

And almost in darkness.

Then she heard the laughter. Uncanny, chilling. It came bursting from the darkness and swept around her. An eerie light appeared before her, coming between the tables where the performers walked to play with their audience.

Someone was playing with her.

In the center of the light was the figure. Black-clad with a mop of yellow hair, faceless, coming toward her. Slowly, then more swiftly, seeming to move without feet.

A scream welled in her throat. Panic seized her. She started to turn toward the door, ready to pound on it and to scream in hysterical terror.

Then somehow, from somewhere, she fought the terror deep inside her.

It was her chance. She didn't believe in specters, and she didn't believe in ghosts. And if anybody knew the truth behind magic and illusion, it should be her. Fantasy was her business.

She had made it her life. She was mistress of all this fantasy herself, and she wasn't going to be duped by tricks of light and darkness.

She turned, shoulders squared, chin firm. "Whoever the hell you are stand still and stop this lunacy! You will not hurt me, and you will not hurt Max, and so help me, I will see that you are locked away from society—and from any trick playing—for a long time!"

The figure wavered. It stood still.

Reggie took a good look at it and started walking forward. "Turn the lights on. Maybe we can discuss this—"

There would be no discussions.

The figure wasn't alone. Reggie hadn't begun to think that the figure might have an accomplice. She had been determined not to panic.

She heard the noise behind her too late. Even as she started to turn, something cracked down on her head.

Then the magic of illusion came to her in truth. Stars, thousands of them, seemed to appear on a black curtain before her.

Then the stars faded. In silence, she crumpled to the ground.

"Reggie, Reggie! For the love of God, speak to me!"

She opened her eyes slowly. For a moment they widened with panic; fear was the first sensation she remembered.

Then she realized that she was lying on the floor in the dino-saloon and that her head was balanced tenderly on Wes's lap. Sharp gold eyes were staring anxiously into hers. His fingers were carefully testing the back of her skull.

She winced when he found the spot where she had been hit.

"Hurt?"

She nodded. Her eyes began to focus better. Max was hunkered down behind Wes.

"And I didn't hit myself in the head!" she assured her brother.

He winced, then offered Wes a half smile. "Well, at least she isn't hurt too badly. She's as nasty as ever."

"I beg your pardon!"

Wes helped her sit up. "We've got an ambulance on the way," he told her.

"An ambulance? I—"

"Reggie, we walked in here and saw you on the floor. My heart came to a complete stop," Wes said firmly. "You're going to the hospital. They're going to take a look at your skull. And Wiler wants to talk to you."

"What happened?" Max asked.

Reggie shook her head. God, did it hurt! For a moment she couldn't remember anything but the fear. Then she remembered that it was her bravado that had gotten her into trouble. "The robotronic person was back. The blond-haired one."

"And the robotronic person hit you in the head?" Wes said.

She shook her head very slowly. The motion hurt. "No. The robotronic wasn't alone. I started yelling something—telling the person that I was going to have him or her arrested. But someone was in back of me."

"And you didn't see who?"

"Not a thing."

She heard footsteps then. Wiler was in the lead, two of his men were behind him, and two paramedics, a young woman and a young man, were behind them.

"Miss Delaney, you do seem to have all sorts of things happening to you," Wiler began angrily.

As if she had wanted someone to conk her on the head!

"It's nice to see you, too, Wiler," she said sweetly. Wes lowered his eyes, grinning, but then he stood and addressed Wiler.

"You want to back off a little? She's been hurt. She needs head X rays."

"But my head is fine!" she protested.

"No, it isn't. It hurts like a son of a bitch," Wes assured her.

"I can't go to a hospital—"

"They'll just keep you overnight. For observation," Wes assured.

"Hey, I'm not waiting for tomorrow to talk to her," Wiler said.

Reggie was trying to rise. The paramedics were beside her, each taking an arm. "Miss Delaney," the young woman said, "you should take it easy. Really."

"Reggie, damn it, go with them!" Max commanded.

"I can't take it easy—"

"I can play dinosaur," Wes assured her. "And you can be out by the saloon show tomorrow afternoon. That is, if you behave decently tonight."

The paramedics had her lying on the stretcher, which they had set on wheels. Wiler was arguing with Max, who was arguing angrily back.

"Wiler, damn it, give him a break, will you?" Wes suddenly exploded. "His sister has just been hurt, his ex-wife is still missing, his place is under some kind of absurd vandalism, and you won't let him breathe! Why isn't someone looking around here, trying to find out what has happened?"

"Oh, I see, Colonel, the military would be handling it better, right?"

"Hell, yes!"

"Well, maybe I'm not looking around because there isn't going to be anything to find!" Wiler said. "And the fingerprints I'm going to get will be from hundreds and hundreds of Mr. and Mrs. Americas!"

"There's surely something—"

"Well, then, you find it, Colonel Army Intelligence!" Wiler said. "This is a loony bin." He turned, staring from Reggie on the stretcher to Max standing above her. "This is some kind of an inside job, and until one of you wants to get straight with me, there just isn't going to be a damn thing to do! Let's hope it happens while you're still living and breathing, Miss Delaney!"

Furious, he stalked off. Max tensed, as if he would go after him, but Wes caught him by the arm. "It's not worth it, Max. It's not worth it."

"Boy, he's mad, isn't he?" the young male paramedic murmured, looking after Wiler. "For my money, the cop hasn't got any right to act that way, Mr. Delaney."

"We did come on a medical emergency," the young woman reminded everyone.

"But it isn't an emergency," Reggie protested. "Two aspirin and a cup of tea—"

"Let's get Reggie in for a checkup, huh?" Wes said. "Max, he's right. We're not going to find anything here. Not now. Reggie is more important."

Reggie kept protesting, but it was all to no avail. She was taken to an ambulance; Max and Wes hung back. She closed her eyes in the ambulance, but the young woman wouldn't let her fall asleep.

"Bad day for you, too, is it?" Reggie asked her.

The paramedic laughed. "Not at all! Your brother offered both Jim—our driver up there—and me year-long passes for entry to the park. It's great! I love the place."

Reggie closed her eyes. "So do I," she said softly.

The young woman squeezed her hand. "Things will straighten out," she promised Reggie.

Reggie hoped so.

But for the moment, they were going to get worse. When she reached the hospital, she found a nurse insisting she put on one of the ridiculous gowns that opened in the back and let a draft chill her to the bone. Barefoot and shivering, she went through a number of X rays. Then she found herself assigned a pleasant young doctor, and then a bed. She did manage to get a private room because Max had been downstairs making the arrangements. Max was with her when the doctor came in to tell her that she had a mild concussion and that they would watch her for the night. Reggie insisted that she didn't want to stay.

"You have to," Max said.

"I don't!"

"You do."

"Why?"

"Because I said so."

"And I'm saying—"

"She's staying," came a voice from the doorway. Wes was there. He exchanged glances with Max and came into the room.

The young doctor leaned back, a grin curling his lip, his arms crossed over his chest. "I can't talk sense to her, and her brother can't talk sense to her. Have you got an idea, sir?"

Wes smiled pleasantly. "Yes. She's staying. Because I'll sit on her if it's necessary to get her to do so."

"Well, that's a relief," the doctor said. He flicked a light into Reggie's eyes, first one then the other, and promised cheerfully that he'd see to it that she got ice cream after dinner. He left, and Max and Wes both burst out with compressed laughter. Reggie would have thrown her pillow at one of them, if she could have decided who she wanted to throw it at more.

"Fine! Laugh!" she told the two of them. But Wes had already sobered. He took a seat by her on the bed, lacing her fingers with his. "Reggie, can you tell us anything more?"

She thought about it for a minute. Then she shook her head. "The person is in costume with a mask and wig. What can I tell you?"

"And what sense does it make to keep plaguing Reggie?" Max asked unhappily.

A nurse's aide walked in with a dinner tray for Reggie. "I'm not hungry—" she began.

"Yes, you are. You do want to leave in the morning, right?" Wes said.

She gritted her teeth. "This is incredible!" she told him.

"Yep. I'm arrogant, bossy and a lot more," he assured her. Then he leaned down to kiss her forehead and added softly, "But remember, I'm ungodly sexy, too." He straightened and looked at her brother. "Max, want to get a bite while Reggie eats?"

"Yeah, sounds good."

They didn't want to eat. They wanted to talk, she thought. And they were going to talk about her. "Hey, you two—" she protested.

But Max gave her a thumbs-up sign and they both disappeared into the hallway.

Half an hour later they were back. Max gave her a kiss good-night. Wes curled into the big comfortable chair by her bed.

"I'm consigned to this miserable place, not you!" she told him.

He was silent for a minute. "Is this where Caleb died?" he asked her.

She nodded.

"Hospitals do good things for people, too, you know," he told her.

"The hospital tried very hard to do good things for Caleb," Reggie said lightly. "It's just the look of the walls, and the bed, and the scent of the place..."

The hospital smelled clean, but it didn't have an overly antiseptic smell to it, Wes thought.

Still, he understood. Reggie hated to come here.

She had to come. It was important to her health.

Still...

What would her health matter if they couldn't understand what was going on? It was true that Daphne had disappeared.

Now all the attacks were against Reggie.

He thought—maybe—that he knew what was going on. Just maybe. But he had to prove it.

And to prove it, he almost needed the attacks on Reggie to continue. His heart leaped and catapulted. He didn't know if he could stand that. Seeing her tonight, so white and ashen and silent on the floor, he had felt as if the insides of his body had been ripped out.

Not Reggie, not this beautiful woman with her spirit and her laughter...

And her magic.

And then she had opened her eyes.

He couldn't risk Reggie. No matter what. He wouldn't leave her alone again.

Not with this going on. Not for a minute.

Her eyes, huge, luminescent, emerald, were on his. "What were you and Max talking about?" she asked him.

"Stock!" he told her cheerfully.

"How can you say that with a smile?" she asked. "Prices must be plummeting. And how can you lie to me like that?"

"Prices are plummeting, but don't worry, I'm buying up whatever I can. And I wasn't lying to you. We were talking about stock," he said. And stockholders, he added silently.

"Mmm," Reggie murmured doubtfully.

"By the way," he told her, determined to get her mind from recent events. "I had lunch today with an old friend who's an attorney."

"Oh?" She frowned, and he knew she was wondering what his words could possibly have to do with anything.

"He's helped any number of couples adopt," Wes said.

Her eyes widened. A shield fell over them. "Illegal adoptions? Adoptions where you have to wait years—"

"He's dealt with adoptions from out of the country, yes, but legal ones," Wes assured her. "But you don't always have to go out of the country. Sometimes, you can opt for a slightly older child. And he told me about lots of possibilities."

Reggie tore her eyes away from his. "You think that I should adopt on my own?" she murmured.

"No, I don't. But I won't just live with you forever, Reggie."

"You've scarcely been living with me a week!" she murmured.

"And a week has been enough. I love you, Reggie. But I won't be some kind of a part-time lover or a stand-in Mr. Delaney. I want marriage."

He saw her eyes glisten. "You're a young man still, Wes—"

"No, I'm an aging old widower, remember?"

"You're a young man!" she insisted softly. "And you may think you love me now, but sometime—"

"Reggie, I'm not all that young, and I'm not stupid, and I happen to like kids. But they don't have to be my own. You think you and Max had it rough. I didn't even know my real father's name until he died, and trust me, it didn't matter then. I told you before—love is what matters. Between a man and a woman, between children and grown-ups. There are a lot of kids in this world who need good parents. Maybe we can salvage life for one of them. You don't have to answer me now—you can think about it."

"I still don't want you giving up your own natural children for me."

"I'm not giving up anything. And I want an answer. You do have a little time."

"How long?"

"At least until tomorrow."

She smiled. He was glad. He had taken her mind off events at the park.

He squeezed her fingers. "Things are going to be all right, Reggie."

She smiled. Her fingers squeezed his back. She closed her eyes.

In a little while he knew that she was sleeping. He smoothed a strand of her beautiful black hair. She'd given him so much. So much magic.

"I'd give up anything for you," he whispered, "and never miss it."

He sat in the chair, leaned back and closed his eyes.

If only he could get his hands on the truth and salvage her magical world . . .

It was probably natural that she should dream that night when she slept. And she did.

She was standing at the end of a long, long aisle. She could see a light, a peculiar, almost heavenly light.

Then she saw that it was coming for her. It had no feet. It drifted. It was black, and it seemed to embody all evil.

Long arms stretched out to her. Arms covered with black, with curious, black-clad fingers that seemed to drip and ooze as if the creature had arisen from some awful kind of muck.

As if the creature had perhaps . . .

Come out of the water.

It kept coming and coming. And she knew that she wanted to accost the creature, but it was screaming at her. It was screaming that she was going to die.

And she could hear the laughter again. The awful, hoarse, cackling laughter. The face was such a blank. Nothing there. Yet there must have been lips somewhere, because the awful thing could talk.

It could threaten.

It could warn her.

It could tell her. . . .

"Reggie, Reggie, Reggie, you're going to die. . . ."

Then the creature's head began to whirl. To whirl and spin, as if it was no longer connected with the body. It couldn't be happening, not in real life, she knew that.

She was dreaming. She had to escape the dream. She had to wake up.

But she couldn't wake up. She could just stare in horror and watch the creature's head spin and try to see more clearly.

There was a mask on one side of the head.

And then . . .

As it turned . . .

She saw Daphne. Daphne's face. Daphne staring at her, Daphne laughing at her.

Promising that she was going to die.

Then the head began to spin faster and faster. . . .

And the words tumbled out, one after another.

"Reggie, Reggie, Reggie . . ."

Spin.

"You're going to, you're going to . . ."

Another spin.

"Die, die, die . . ."

Chapter 12

She woke up, trying to hold back a scream, a soft sob escaping her.

She nearly jumped, amazed at how fast warm, strong arms came around her. She was shaking. Wes held her tight. The shaking began to subside. She leaned her head back. She had come to know the subtle, sexy male scent of him so well. She knew the feel of his arms so well.

If he were to leave her now...

And yet she believed with her whole heart that to hold on to him would be wrong.

That was something she was going to have to think about later.

"I was dreaming," she said quickly. "I woke you, I'm sorry."

"I'm not surprised you were dreaming," he said. "And I really wasn't sleeping all that great in that chair, anyway."

"Uncomfortable?" she whispered.

"No, it's your outfit. It's that hospital nightgown with the squat little blue people all over it."

She smiled.

"No, really, it is the nightgown. It's the way the slit keeps falling open in the back. I keep telling myself about all the things I could be doing to your back—and your front—if we were home."

Home. He had said home.

She smiled. "You insisted that I say here."

His fingers threaded through her hair. It was damp. The dream had been a seriously scary one. He knew it.

"What happened?"

"The creature was coming after me again."

"And?"

"And then it turned into Daphne. It was like one of those change-o things they used to give away at the fast-food restaurants. One side of the head was the masked and wigged robotronic. The other side of the head was Daphne. And she was laughing and cackling and promising that I was going to die. Sounds pretty ridiculous, huh?"

He didn't answer her right away. His arms tightened around her.

"Not with your imagination," he assured her.

"Hey. If you're making fun of me—"

"I'm not!" He laughed hastily. His arms were around her. His chin rested on her head. She suddenly had the idea that he wasn't telling her something, but what it could be, she didn't know. And she could wait. She felt a rush of warmth from his touch, and she, too, was wishing that they were home. She turned in his arms. His hand brushed over her naked breast, beneath the soft cotton of the funny hospital gown. He groaned and withdrew the intimate touch quickly.

"Behave, you wicked temptress! Trying to seduce me in a hospital bed, eh?"

"No!" The dream was fading quickly. And still, there was something speculative about his golden gaze, even as he made her laugh.

"There's nothing wrong with your imagination," he told her softly, and kissing her forehead, he eased her back on the bed. "You're the mistress of magic, and your imagination has made a haven for all sorts of wounded souls!" he assured her.

Not to mention his own!

"Try to get some more sleep. I'll be here."

She smiled, closed her eyes and slept.

She did so knowing that he would keep his word, always.

He would be at her side.

In the morning, he barely pecked her cheek before leaving. He had to get to the park—after all, he had promised to play a dinosaur.

Reggie waited impatiently until almost ten o'clock when the doctor came and decided to release her with a sheet of symptoms that she must watch out for and with a severe warning.

Meekly, eyes downcast, she promised the doctor that she would be good.

He said she could go right after lunch.

At twelve-thirty Diana came to pick her up and the two women tried to understand what they could about everything that had happened.

"Maybe Daphne is alive," Diana said. "You said your figure might be the right size and height."

"But she's not in this alone," Reggie said.

"No."

"So what's the point to the whole thing?"

"It seems like the destruction of the park—through Max," Diana said.

"Maybe," Reggie agreed.

"So what do we do?" Diana murmured.

"We just keep fighting it," Reggie said. "The best that we can."

"You," Diana warned her, "had best quit fighting it! Who knows what will happen next time?"

A shiver danced up and down Reggie's spine. "Well, I've been given very strict orders not to be alone. I'll be careful."

"I thought you were being careful before."

"I'll be more careful."

She didn't need to worry too much that afternoon. In the middle of the show, she realized that Wes was in the audience.

She came down the aisle and sat on his lap and mussed his hair, and did her very, very best tormenting him.

But Wes wouldn't be so easily had.

He caught her by the middle, flipped her over his arm and stole a long, passionate kiss. Breathless, Reggie told Bob that he had best find someone else to marry.

The audience loved it. Bob sighed and told her that she had to marry him, it was in the script.

But when the show was over, Wes was waiting, and she went home with him. And the moment they were in the doorway he was asking her if she really didn't have a headache that night.

She assured him that she didn't.

He had aches, he told her.

"Terrible aches?" she asked him.

"The worst. But you can fix them."

"All?"

"Every one of them."

She did so, kissing his lips, his cheeks, his forehead. On the stairway she undid the little pearl snaps on his shirt and pressed her lips against the platinum furred expanse of his chest. Then she found herself in his arms, and very soon after, in her bedroom. He held her close and kissed her, and she slipped her fingers into the waistband of his snug jeans, running her touch along the small of his back.

She heard the scratch of a zipper being quickly ripped open, and his jeans were on the floor. His hands were on her hips and she was flying backward to the bed. Smiling, she moved her hands through his hair.

"The socks are a wonderful touch!" she told him.

"Hey! I still can't get that hospital gown out of my mind!" he retorted.

She laughed. She caught his cheeks in her hands, and she kissed him, tasting his lips, nibbling, experimenting.

But then she felt the hardness of his arousal against her naked flesh, and in seconds he was filling her, and she lost all thought of teasing and of play. The need overrode all else, and a rising fire ignited deep inside her. It burst upon her brilliantly. While she was still savoring the sensations, her phone began to ring.

"Leave it," Wes told her.

"I can grab it. It's right here," she murmured, rolling over to catch the receiver.

"Hello?"

"Is Wes Blake there, please?" a voice asked.

A feminine voice. A soft, hushed voice.

But very definitely a woman's.

She frowned. The voice sounded familiar. No, not really. She didn't know it. Not the way it sounded, so soft. Muffled.

Something about it bothered her, though.

"Is he there?" Impatient. Worried.

"Yes, just a moment, please."

She handed the phone to Wes. He arched a brow at her. She shrugged, scooting over to one side of the bed while he spoke.

Actually, he spoke very little. He said, "Hello," then a few minutes later he said, "All right." And then, "Yeah, yeah, all right, you know me."

She couldn't gauge his reaction to the caller because his back was to her while he spoke.

"What was it?" Reggie asked.

He shrugged, his back still to her. "Just one of the clerks from the police station. She's gotten a few more pages of information for me on stockholders I couldn't get much on." He rolled across the bed, returning the receiver to her. She hung up the receiver, wondering why she didn't believe his answer.

"Really?" she asked.

Was there just a beat before he answered her?

"Really," he said. "Hungry?"

"Mmm."

"Good. Let's get something to eat." He kissed her. The kiss lengthened. And lengthened. She felt his muscles tightening.

Then she felt the hardening against her thigh once again. She smiled and touched him. Fingers stroking, then curving around him. He groaned softly, his face darkening, tightening. She began innocently enough. "Wes, I thought that you wanted—"

"I did."

"But if you want—"

"I do want, you little sorceress!"

"I'm referring to a meal!" she said, wide-eyed.

"Mmm. And I plan to feast."

"Then—"

"This first," he assured her firmly, golden eyes gleaming.

"You said you were really hungry."

"You betcha."

"Then—"

"Certain tastes just blind out all others," he murmured.

"Oh..."

Two could play the same game. His hands were on her. Stroking. Intimate. Caressing.

"There are just so many ways to be hungry!" he whispered against her flesh.

Yes, oh, yes...

She rolled to her stomach. He kissed her nape. Moving. Sliding down the length of her back. Teasing the small of her back. His hands were smoothing her buttocks. She was rolling again. Feeling the sweet wet heat of his caress.

"Oh, so hungry!" she whispered.

His lips claimed hers.

His body did the same.

She forgot all about the phone call.

Four days later she was sitting in her office when she was buzzed from within the park. She picked up the receiver to find Rick Player was on the phone.

"What the hell is going on now?" he demanded angrily.

Reggie looked at the phone. "I don't know, Rick. What the hell is going on?"

"You'd better find out, and find out fast, or I'll demand another emergency meeting of the board. This is all getting out of hand."

"What is getting out of hand?"

"Read your copy of the *Tell-All News*. There's one in your In box—I dropped it off this morning. I'll be back with you in a few minutes."

She didn't have a few minutes, she wanted to tell him, but he had already hung up. She reached into her box and found the paper he had left. She gasped as she saw the front page.

"Ghost Of Ex-Delaney Bride Terrorizes Dinosaur Theme Park!"

She set down the paper, furious. Who had known about her experiences? Just her, Max, Wes, Diana— and Wiler. Well, if Wiler knew, everyone at the police station might know. And some people just couldn't resist a juicy story—whether it was true or not.

She read quickly through the article. "Sources" close to the park and the events taking place had reported that Daphne's "ghost" had appeared to a number of people, including Regina Delaney.

And of course, there was a wonderful, poetic justice to it all. No matter how big Max Delaney thought he was, his poor ex-wife was managing to get her revenge.

"Oh, she's getting it all right!" Reggie murmured. She set the paper down, drumming her fingers on the desk. Then she realized that the article went on. She flipped the page.

She gasped again. Covering an entire page was a photo of Daphne with a man.

The man wasn't Max.

It was Wesley Blake.

Cold seemed to steal over her, like pellets of ice water dripping over her from melting snow above a frozen stream.

Daphne was with Wes. His arm was around her. She was dressed in sequins; he was in a magnificent tux. The caption beneath the photo said that Daphne was attending a fund-raiser with heart-stopping tycoon Wesley Blake in San Francisco.

The article went on to talk about Daphne's fun-loving life-style and bubbling personality until she had settled down with Max. And then it quoted Daphne as saying that Max Delaney, creator, genius, was really none other than one of his creations himself—an absolute monster.

It was damning press. Damning.

And she was furious. Really furious. And she was worried about Max.

The cold left her. Fury, hot, irrational, swept through her.

Wes.

Why hadn't he told her? They had talked about everyone in Daphne's past and present. Wes had listened to her. He had spent endless days at the police station, endless days prowling through the park.

Max was a suspect; Reggie herself had been a suspect.

And he had never even mentioned that he and Daphne had been on such friendly terms.

Her door flew open. Rick Player stood there, angry, smug. He walked across the room and sat on the corner of the desk and leaned toward her. He tapped the photo with his finger. "Nice shot of Blake, eh?"

She didn't answer him. Her fingers were trembling.

She suddenly realized who the voice of the woman on the phone belonged to.

It was Daphne's voice.

Chapter 13

It was almost impossible for Reggie to calm down enough to handle the rest of the day, and yet, with the awful story out in the press, she had to wade her way through it with a level head.

Her first difficulty was in trying to get Rick Player out of her office.

"So you'll go to dinner with Blake and not with me?" Rick persisted.

"Rick, I'll go to dinner with you—sometime."

He sat on the edge of her desk, leaning closer. "Why not tonight?"

"I have a lot of work to do."

"I just want dinner first. I'm sure Blake wanted a whole lot more. And from the looks of things, he got what he wanted."

Anger washed over her in great waves. She clenched her teeth, cast her head back at a controlled angle and managed to refrain from hitting him. "If you aren't out of here in two seconds, I'll call my brother."

Player smiled. "And what's he going to do—kill me?"

"Get out. I wouldn't go to dinner with you in a thousand years after the things you just said, Rick. Now, go, please."

He wagged a finger at her. "You'll be sorry. I promise, you'll be sorry for this."

When he was gone, she groaned and leaned her head on the desk.

What had she done to deserve this?

Rick Player had been after her for years. He had never bothered her. He had been after anyone young, halfway attractive and female for those same years.

Wesley. Wesley with Daphne. That bothered her.

First things first.

She swallowed her anger and pride and began to call the major papers. As always she started with Fran Rainier. She tried to make light of the entire thing at first, but then she heard Fran sigh deeply.

"So just what is going on down there?"

"Someone is playing tricks in the shops," Reggie admitted after a moment. "Fran, honestly, there is no ghost running around the park." She hesitated. "Fran, why don't you come down here? A working vacation. We'll put you up at—" She hesitated. The park owned three lodging facilities. Which would Fran like the best? "I know! You could bring your grandsons. We'll give you a little suite at the Plesiosaur Pad. The kids will love it. I don't know if you've seen it or not, but it has one of those theme pools. There's a water slide that resembles the Loch Ness monster, and all kinds of wonderful things—"

"And you're bribing me," Fran told her firmly.

"Yes, of course. Fran, I've never asked you not to print anything that was true. And if you're here, you'll know what is happening firsthand. And—and anything I get that I can give you, I'll make exclusive until the other papers pick it up from you."

"I'll be there just as soon as I can round up the boys. The place has a golf course, I assume? If you're bribing me, I want it first class all the way."

"Aye, there'll be a wee golf course!" Reggie promised. "We'll have you in the concierge tower and you'll just love it, I promise."

"And I get an exclusive, right?"

"Right," Reggie promised.

"I'll be there tonight."

Reggie pushed the disconnect button, then started to dial the hotel to make the arrangements. She pushed the button again. She'd run over to the hotel herself. She started dialing again, this time gritting her teeth when she heard the voice on the other end.

"Ozzie Daniels here."

Reggie could picture him. He was of medium height and medium build. He couldn't have been more than thirty-five or forty, and he might even have been an attractive man, but his face was hard and unfriendly. He reminded her of a wolverine. Vicious and dangerous, in his way.

"Mr. Daniels," she said coolly. "This is Regina Delaney. I'm ever so curious about where you came up with this absurd story about ghosts in our park."

She heard a soft chuckle at the other end. "It was a good story, huh?"

"I thought that newspaper reporters were supposed to deal with facts," Reggie said.

"I give 'em like I see 'em," he told her.

"And if you don't give them straight," Reggie warned him softly, "you're going to wind up with a lawsuit on your hands."

"Oh, come on, now, Reggie, there are a lot of people who would love to come to a park with ghosts!"

She hated him to call her Reggie. The only person Ozzie Daniels began to compare with in the slime factor was Rick Player.

"You've maligned my brother with no proof," she said bluntly. "You've tried to destroy a place that has been a haven for children. You've—"

"You've never made the least effort to give me a quarter-inch column, Miss Delaney. You think that you and your high-and-mighty brother are better than I—"

"We're better than the trash you sling in that paper!" Reggie said furiously.

She heard his soft chuckle again and bit her lip. He was so pleased to have disturbed her. "Why, honey, you and your brother are making the trash for me to print! Wait until you see tomorrow's paper!"

"Wait a minute! What are you—"

"How'd you like the picture display, Reggie? After all, you are picking up where Daphne left off."

"What the hell—"

"Ooh! She's perfect, she's beautiful, she's talented, she's the darling of a nation. And she swears like a truck driver!" Ozzie crooned over the phone.

She wanted to swear like a truck driver. She wanted to call him every name in the book. She fought for control and told him in a voice that dripped frozen venom, "I swear, Mr. Daniels, I will see you in court."

"Court! You can only sue if you prove that what I've printed is libel. And I'm watching what I say! I'm watching it very carefully. But I'll tell you what. Let's have dinner. We'll talk."

"Dinner!"

"Yes, it's a meal—"

"Daniels, I can't begin to see stomaching a meal in your presence." She bit her lip. What was this with dinner? Couldn't someone be original and suggest breakfast? Or was dinner just the best meal because people usually went home after it, and because it could last forever?

"Then maybe you shouldn't eat," Ozzie said bitterly. "Cut me some slack. Maybe I could print better things if I got something from you now and then."

"Mr. Daniels—"

"I know. You're too good for this paper. But let me remind you—people love this kind of thing. They lap it up. And my circulation is in the millions, Miss Delaney."

Reggie hesitated. She hated him. Absolutely hated him.

Then again, he was the one who had discovered that Daphne was missing.

Except that now she was certain Daphne wasn't missing, after all.

And Wes knew it. And Wes had dated Daphne. And he had probably had quite an affair with her. . . .

And no one had bothered to tell Reggie.

"I'll meet you at eight o'clock tonight," she heard herself promise.

"Where? Someone dark and romantic—"

"Harry's Hot Dog Stand, on the highway."

A sigh. A very deep sigh. "I'll be there."

She set the phone down as if the receiver might bite her.

Harry's Hot Dog Stand was hardly a den of iniquity, but still . . .

She felt a little slimy.

It didn't matter. Ozzie wanted information from her.

She wanted information from Ozzie.

Reggie spent most of the morning torn between an awful chill and a red hot fury.

She'd been falling in love.

No.

She was in love. And everything about him had seemed wonderful. That was why it was so terrible to feel betrayed to the core. She had loved him, did love him, hated him . . .

There could be an explanation, she tried to tell herself. What explanation could there be? Pictures could tell stories more vividly than words. And there he was in that picture, handsome—and apparently even charming!—with Daphne on his arm.

Argh!

Making it through the day was pure torture.

Being a dinosaur was pure torture.

She tried to tell herself that there was a very positive side to this whole affair. Daphne was alive, she was certain. That was positive. It was wonderful. Max couldn't be guilty of murder.

But Wes was guilty of—something!

After her stint as a dinosaur Reggie hurried over to the hotel to make the arrangements for Fran Rainier. Dierdre's DinoLand owned the property and fifty percent interest in the hotel while a large chain held the other half interest as a silent partner. She and Max had always liked the arrangement because they were good at the creative part of management, while the hotel people really knew their stuff. She'd learned a bit about the hotel and restaurant business because of their association. One of the things she had learned was that graciousness was a must—and that it was true, even when a customer was wrong, or way out of line at the very least, the customer had to be considered right.

At the hotel, they bent over backward for the comfort of the guests.

Reggie took a minute to admire the pool. She and Max had done the preliminary sketches—then the pool people had taken over. It was really a watery wonderland. There was a sand pool with tropical fish, and there was the theme pool where little dinosaurs with caps **like** those on the Loch Ness monster arose from the watery depths to shoot sprays of water at frolicking children.

There was a quieter lap pool, and there was the sports pool, a large rectangular creation with volleyball nets and basketball hoops and all kinds of sports-oriented enticements.

She made a mental note that when things were all over, when Max was in the clear and when Wes Blake was in a plane heading for San Francisco—and when she'd had a chance to dump a gallon of ice water on Daphne's head—she'd spend a week here herself.

In the concierge tower she made the arrangements for Fran. Jeannie Talmadge, the manager of the concierge level, promised her that Fran would want for nothing. "Come and see the guest lounge," she encouraged Reggie. Then, her high black heels making a soft clicking sound on marble flooring, she led Reggie to double French doors that opened into a large room with cozy groups of handsome Victorian furniture. Huge windows opened to the pools far below and the boat arenas on Lake Plesiosaur. It was a spectacular sight.

"We're getting ready for cocktail hour. Coconut shrimp, conch fritters, cheese, crab-stuffed mushrooms, and that's just tonight. The buffet breakfast has all kinds of eggs, bacon, sausage, salmon...you name it. And the desserts later in the evenings! If I were to weaken here just one night, I could be rolled home!"

Reggie doubted it. Jeannie was a lean, attractive brunette, a business major, and a no-nonsense woman but still a very warm one.

"So, you're going to feed her into submission!" Reggie said.

Jeannie grinned. "Hey, why not? It's worth a try. Besides, it's not bribery—it's the way we treat all our guests. And I don't think we need to bribe Fran. Fran believes in the magic, and she knows what you and Max have done."

"Thanks!" Reggie told her. "She's coming in tonight sometime. I'll call her early in the morning to see
her."

"Why don't you just come here?"

"That's not a bad idea. Tell her I'll meet her here in
the morning. About eight, if that's not too early for
her. If it is, she can call me at home—er, no." She had
a dinner date at eight. At Harry's Hot Dog Stand. She
might not be home until late.

And then there was the matter of Wes Blake....

Just thinking of him brought a trembling to her
fingers and a downward plunge to her heart. How
could he betray her so? And Max?

Just what was going on?

She closed her eyes, remembering his words. Love
was what mattered. Love was what mattered....

Children mattered. She knew, because she knew
how badly she wanted her own. She knew how badly
she had wanted them with Caleb. Children were wonderful. They were the real magic of the world.

But Wes hadn't seemed to care. He'd sounded as if
he doubted anyone could love an adopted child any
the less.

The love was what mattered....

As if love really existed.

And if she dared to think of the days and nights
gone past between them, she would make herself
crazy.

"Reggie?"

Jeannie was looking at her with a concerned frown.
"Sorry! There's so much to think about these days."

"I guess so. It must be just awful for you and Max.
All that horrible press. But Reggie, remember, any-

one who knows you and Max—or even knows anything about you and Max—knows that this is all just a big mistake. If Daphne did come to harm, it wasn't through Max!"

"Thanks. But you know what? I have this feeling that Daphne is really all right."

"You do?"

Yes, because I'm positive I heard her voice, Reggie thought. Because she called the man living with me, my lover . . .

A man who may still be her lover!

"Yes, I think she's all right," she said. "Daphne is certainly capable of a stunt like this. Well, I'd best get going. I have a show this afternoon."

And I have to tell a conniving, two-timing, devious blackguard exactly where to go! she reminded herself.

After she told him she knew Daphne was alive . . .

And demand that he produce her.

Wes was seated by one of the saloon beams when the show started.

He didn't want her to see him at first.

Joseph was seated to his left.

The little boy was eight years old, nearly nine. He was a beautiful child. His eyes were blue, a clear blue like the color of the sky. His hair was yellow blond, a little long, a little shaggy.

And he was tough. Life had made him that way. But despite the toughness, there was also something innately courteous, warm and gentle about him. When Wes had told him they were going to spend the day in the park, his eyes had widened. He still believed in magic. No matter what life had done, he still believed in magic.

For Wes, that was the clincher.

He really didn't have the time to be doing things on a personal level at the moment—there was Daphne, and whatever the hell was going on with her, to be reckoned with. But Daphne had steadfastly refused to say anything other than when she would meet him. She had sworn vociferously that her life was in danger, that he was the only one she could really trust.

So he had to hang on.

And while he was delving into files, he had come across Joseph's picture.

Actually he had been going through some of Max's files—with Max's permission—when he had found the folder on the boy. It had intrigued him, so he had pulled it out. The picture had caught his heart right away—those big blue eyes and the look that he would defy the world. "Who's this?" he'd asked Max.

"He was going to be my next special guest at the park."

"And that means?" Wes prompted.

"Reggie and I do a lot with various foundations. For disabled children, children with life-threatening diseases and with orphans. That's Joseph Brennan. He falls into the last category. It's a sad story. He was supposed to have been adopted at birth, but the couple insisted on a girl. Can you imagine that? A beautiful baby like that—and they wouldn't take him? Anyway, he wound up being shifted around, he went to a few foster homes, and suddenly he was past the age most couples want a child to be when they adopt. He lived with an elderly aunt for a few years, but then she became too ill to keep him. Anyway, the woman at the children's shelter knows how Reggie and I feel about little ones like this, so she sent me the file. I was getting ready to bring it to Reggie when all this stuff broke and it didn't seem to be the time for special guests."

"Would you mind if I went to see him and maybe brought him over?"

"No. Of course not. I'd be delighted. It's just that, with me under this cloud of suspicion, I didn't know what else I might be accused of!"

"Would Reggie mind?"

Max looked at him sharply. "If you're planning—"

"I'm planning on asking your sister to marry me," Wes interrupted quickly, and was rewarded with a broad, relieved grin from his friend. "And I know how she feels about children, and that she can't have her own—"

Max sighed. "No one told Reggie that she absolutely can't have her own. What the doctor said was that she had a severely tilted uterus and that it might not be possible for her to conceive. And then she was with Caleb for years before the accident, always hoping..." He shrugged. "So it doesn't look good." Max straightened his shoulders. He was suddenly the older brother—by five minutes—determined to protect his sister. "Don't marry her in hopes that things can change, Wes. It would hurt her worse—"

Wes tapped the picture. "Max, how the hell long have you known me? And after the way we both grew up, how can you question how I might feel toward adopted children?"

Max looked stunned. "You're thinking of adopting this boy?"

"Of course not! It's not that easy! I'm planning on picking him up. On bringing him to the park. On getting to know him. On introducing him to Reggie."

Max had been standing. He plopped into the seat behind his desk. "You're serious."

Wes grinned. "Look at the puss on that kid, Max. Who does he remind you of?"

Max smiled suddenly. "Me at that age," he said softly. He looked at Wes. "You?"

"Yep. Of course, we all have to get to know each other first. And I haven't even formally asked Reggie to marry me. And she can be so damned stubborn."

Max waved a hand in the air. Suddenly, it was all right for Wes to handle Reggie any way he wanted. "Drag her to the altar. I'll help you."

"Thanks!"

"There's still this matter of Daphne," Max said irritably.

"She's terrified of someone," Wes said, sitting on the edge of Max's desk. "I can only pray that she really meets me—and that my hunch is right. You didn't tell Reggie anything, did you?"

"No! I want her far from the action when it happens. Daphne swears she wasn't trying to hurt Reggie. And she won't say anything more until she's convinced that she's safe."

"I just pray it's over shortly."

"Then I'll tell Reggie everything."

There was a lot Wes wanted to tell Reggie that he hadn't told her yet. He wanted to make her see his past life so that she would believe in him, really believe in him. He didn't want her refusing him the way she had refused Caleb. And he wanted her to believe that he'd be giving up nothing if he left San Francisco behind and moved here. He wasn't an artist. He did know a hell of a lot about business management and security. Max was anxious for him to stay. He hoped that Reggie would feel the same.

She was just now appearing on the stage in the garish red dress and the black fishnet stockings. She was singing about the benefit of her evil ways in such a funny fashion that the audience was vibrant with laughter. Wes watched Joseph. The hardened little tyke had his eyes set hard on Reggie.

"That's her?" he said to Wes.

"Yep. Reggie Delaney. She drew the first Dierdre Dinosaur and made a puppet out of her when she was just about your age. Don't you think that's fun?"

Joseph stared at Wes with his wide blue eyes. "Yeah, well, it's all right. You've gotta understand, a lot of the guys my age think puppets are kind of sissy." He smiled suddenly. "Except that everyone was impressed that I got to come here. The rides are awesome. And—" He hesitated a minute, looking at Reggie. "She's really beautiful. Does she always dress like that?"

Wes cuffed Joseph lightly on the head.

Actually, the fishnet stockings and garish red made up one of his very favorite outfits for Reggie, one he thought of with great affection.

"Naw, it's just a costume. You know that."

Joseph grinned. He liked to lead grown-ups along, but it was in good fun. He had a tough armor, but there was a lot inside that was still soft and gentle. So

far, he'd eaten hot dogs and ice cream with an amazing capacity, and right after, he'd gone on the worst of
the dino-twisters without blinking when Wes had been
praying that he wouldn't throw up himself. Puppets
might be sissy, but Joseph was having a heck of a good
time with them anyway.

"Look, here she comes," Wes said.

Reggie was on her way down the aisle. The boa was
fluffing over various faces in the audience. She
stopped and chatted here and there with a delight-
fully funny sleazy accent, then moved on.

Wes backed up behind the support beam and
watched as she came across Joseph.

Yes, he did, he knew Reggie.

He watched as her elegant green eyes widened and
softened. A slow smile curved her lips, and she ruf-
fled his hair with her boa. "Well, now, this one here
is a handsome one!" she called back to Bob. "Maybe
we can get a ransom on him. What do you say, son?
You gotta mind to ride off on a dinosaur into the sun-
set?"

Joseph was laughing, but he quickly assured Reggie, "You can't get any ransom on me, Miss Patricia.
There's no one to pay it."

Wes saw the emotion flick through her eyes. She
knew instantly that the boy wasn't lying. "Hmm!" she
said, skipping only a beat. "Guess we'll just have to
keep this one, Bob!" She whirled around. "Well,
there's just gotta be some old—or young!—geezer out
here to make some kind of a profit off!"

"You're slipping, Patricia!" Bob called to her.

"Oh, do leave them all alone!" Alise said in a syr-
upy sweet young heroine's voice. "Miss Patricia, you

are supposed to be reforming Bob and yourself and going on to lead a good life.''

''Oh, I will, I will! Eventually!'' Reggie promised. ''It's just such a big world. And so many men!''

She turned again.

She started to sit on Wes's lap.

Then she saw his face, even as she landed warmly on his lap.

Wes began to smile.

But then, to his absolute amazement, Reggie hauled off and slapped him. Right across the face.

There was silence in the audience.

And silence on the stage.

Bob broke the silence. ''I don't think that's the way to get money out of him, honey.''

Thankfully, the audience started to laugh then, convinced that Wes had to be part of the show. In the roar that followed Wes jerked her close to him. ''What the hell was that for?''

But she was already up, turning away. ''Some you kiss, and some you slap. You've just gotta keep 'em on their toes!'' she announced, hurrying to the stage.

Bob stepped down. He was proposing to Reggie. They were going to lead a good life at last. The show was almost over.

Joseph looked at Wes politely. ''Are you absolutely sure that she likes you?''

''Funny, kid, funny,'' Wes murmured. He stroked his cheek. It stung.

''Does she always greet you like that?''

The show was over; the audience was filing out.

He shook his head. ''No. You wait here for a minute. It will be all right. I'll be right back, okay?''

"Sure. This is your ball game, mister," Joseph said matter-of-factly.

"Don't leave, all right?"

Joseph grinned. "Hey, I want to come back. The rides are fun, the food is great. And you're all right."

"Thanks," Wes acknowledged.

He left Joseph sitting at the table and hurried around back. He was going to have to hope that Alise would forgive him bursting into the dressing room because that was exactly what he intended to do.

But he didn't have to. Reggie was already on her way out. He hadn't even gotten backstage before he ran right into her.

"Excuse me!" she told him icily. "I have things to do."

She was going to try to walk right by him!

He caught her arm. Caught it firmly. "What the hell is this all about?" he demanded.

"I haven't time to talk about it now."

"Well, I have time now. All the time in the world."

"Let go of me."

"No."

"I can scream—"

"Go right ahead. This is your park, remember?"

Her eyes flashed a wild, emerald fire. She was shaking with emotion.

But she wasn't going to scream. She stood still, her jaw rock hard, twisted and set. "You tell me what's going on. Mr. Blake, are you just like the others? Like Player and Ozzie Daniels? You all had fixations on Max's wife—now you're turning them on his sister?"

"What?" he demanded sharply.

"Don't lie!" she snapped. "Why the hell didn't you tell me you'd been sleeping with Daphne?"

So that was it. How had she learned about it?

Maybe he should have apologized right away. Something inside him rebelled. After everything, she should have trusted him a little.

"I've slept with a number of women. I didn't know that I was required to give you a roster of their names."

"Daphne!" she stressed, her eyes narrowing.

"I knew her before your brother did, but there was really very little between us. They hit it off right away."

"So you lied to Max, too—"

"No, Miss Delaney, Max knew the score right from the beginning."

Her eyes narrowed further. "Right. And Max married her. And Max is accused of killing her. But she's alive—and you're the one she calls!"

Damn. She'd recognized Daphne's voice, even muffled. He should have told her.

He just didn't want her getting hurt. Didn't want her there when he tried to meet Daphne tonight.

"Damn it, Reggie—"

"Get out of my way, Wes."

"Yeah, you're right, Reggie. I'll get out of your way. You just judge blindly, and nothing that's been said or done matters. Fine."

She started to walk past him. His fingers tightened around her arm.

"Reggie—"

"I've got things to do!" she claimed.

She strained against him. This time he let her break free.

He heard the doors to the theater slam as she left.

A moment later, Joseph was behind him. "I don't know, Mr. Blake. I wouldn't want to hurt your feelings or anything, but I really don't think she likes you."

"She loves me, kid."

"Sure, if you say so."

"Mmm, and she'll say so, too. Just as soon as I get a chance to see her alone. To give a good—"

He broke off, looking at Joseph.

"A good shaking."

Joseph grinned. "Actually, I think you'd do a hell of a lot better if you'd kiss her. And you should have told her that you were sleeping with Daphne."

"Yeah, and I should wash your mouth out with soap."

Joseph offered Wes a hand. "It's gonna work out. I have a feeling. But stick with the kissing. Trust me, I know."

"Oh, yeah? And just how do you know?"

He smiled. "Trust me!"

Wes felt his temper ease. *She's going to like you so much, kid, if she'll just give us both the chance!* he thought. He smiled. But then his smile faded.

Where was she heading?

Daphne was still alive.

But Reggie was still in danger.

He paled. He had to get someone to watch Joseph for the moment.

Because he didn't dare let Reggie get too far ahead of him.

God alone knew just what she might do.

Chapter 14

Harry's Hot Dog Stand was well lit, almost blindingly so. Reggie had admitted to herself that she had been a little worried about meeting Ozzie Daniels—she wasn't exactly sure why—but once she reached the painfully bright fast-food restaurant, she felt much more at ease.

And Ozzie was there, waiting for her.

He was nicely dressed, and if she hadn't known him, she might have thought that he was a fairly appealing individual.

But she did know him.

He met her at the door. "How do you like your franks?" he asked immediately. He looked like a reporter. He was wearing a dark trench coat over a dark suit. Maybe it was supposed to rain. Reggie wasn't sure.

"I can get—"

"Oh, come on, Miss Delaney. Surely, you'll allow me the honor of buying you your franks! After all, the dinner invitation was mine."

She shook her head. "I'm just not hungry. I was going to get a soda and an order of curly fries. You're more than welcome to get them for me, if you like."

She waited at one of the bleached white Formica tables while he went for the food. When he came back, he had her fries and soda and three hot dogs for himself, one piled high with chili, one with sauerkraut and one with melted cheese. He grimaced at her. "I couldn't make up my mind," he told her. She almost smiled.

If he weren't out for Max's jugular, she might not have disliked him so intensely.

"There's no one haunting the park," she told him.

He arched a brow and bit into one of his dogs. "Getting right to business. Not, how are you Ozzie, what ya been up to, or anything of the like."

"You've been up to maligning my brother and the park. What do you want from me?"

He shook his head. "Not much, I guess. All right, no one is haunting the park. So what is going on?"

Reggie shook her head. "I don't really know. But I'll tell you something—I don't think that my brother could possibly be guilty of Daphne's murder."

"And why is that?"

"I don't believe that Daphne's dead."

His left brow flew up. Was it an act? Or did he know that Daphne was alive and well? Had he been in on this with her?

After all, he was the one who had discovered her missing....

He was either innocent, or a very good actor.

He lifted his root-beer bottle and drank from it. "You should have seen her apartment."

"I did."

He shrugged. "Well, who knows. So what is going on in the park?"

"Just a prankster, nothing more."

"Would you care to go on about that?"

She shrugged, as casual as she could possibly be. "Someone was dressing up like one of the robotronics. It was silly, really."

"See, the way that I heard it," Ozzie told her, "Daphne came flying out of the darkness—after you. Or Daphne's ghost."

"No ghosts were after me."

"Just cute little snuggly dinosaurs, right?"

"I told you—"

"You called the police."

"Of course. We frown upon pranksters in the park."

"You're not giving me anything, Reggie."

"Yes, I am. I'm giving you the truth. Want to try to print it for a change?"

To her surprise, he glanced at his watch instead of pressing her. "Did you like the picture of your boyfriend?" he asked her suddenly.

Her fingers tightened around her soda bottle. She hoped she didn't give anything away with her expression. "Wes is a handsome man," she said softly. "He always photographs well."

"And Daphne was—is—beautiful."

"Daphne is very beautiful."

"Maybe they're in this thing together."

"For what?" Reggie asked him.

He smiled. She had given something away. He touched her fingers where they lay on the table. "Wes Blake discredits your brother. He's got big bucks. Your brother steps aside, Wes Blake steps in. Then he's got it all, lock, stock and barrel. He even has the boss man's wife."

"Gosh. And I had rather thought you were busy coveting Daphne yourself," Reggie said lightly.

"Ah, but then there's Rick Player."

"Yes, there is."

"So?"

He left the question open, grinning. Then she noticed that he glanced at his watch again. He did have another appointment. Well, so much about being concerned for her virtue. She could have picked any spot to meet him.

"I'd better get going," she said, baiting him.

"Yeah. Yeah, well, me, too. I'm glad you met with me, Reggie. I appreciate it. And I'll try to print what you've told me."

She nodded and watched him walk out, puzzled. Then she jumped up suddenly, determined to follow him.

He was leaving the parking lot as she reached it. She hopped quickly into her car and drove onto the highway, following him.

For some reason, it didn't surprise her terribly to find that he was headed toward the park.

Reggie did likewise.

She was able to keep almost directly behind him until she began to come to the lanes for the park. There was one for parking, one for employees, one for the hotel and one for buses. Reggie swore softly as she realized that she had lost him.

She pulled to the side of the road, frustrated for a minute. She leaned her head back. She had met with him. She had told him all kinds of stuff—with and without words. And she hadn't learned a thing about Wes and Daphne.

With a sigh she brought her motor to life, ready to turn around and go home. She knew that she was going to have a real live argument with Wes, the kind she couldn't walk out on.

Either that...

Or he wouldn't be there at all. Not after the way she had acted today.

She realized suddenly that she had started the car and that she was driving very mechanically into the employee parking lot.

She was about to turn around when she realized that Max's car was still in the lot.

So was Wesley's.

She drove up beside Max's car and parked.

When she approached the entrance to the park, she noticed that there was no guard on duty there.

Was security slipping?

"Hello!" she cried out.

Even the cleaning crews were gone. Her voice echoed eerily in the stucco cave. Where was everyone?

Reggie slipped through one of the turnstiles. Where were Max and Wes? Her heart was thumping, and she tried to assure herself that there was certainly no reason for either of them to be at the front of the park, expecting her.

Reggie tried the door to the front offices. It was locked. She had her keys and could have opened it, but if Max or Wes had been upstairs, the door wouldn't have been locked.

Maybe they were in their private offices.

She tried the next door. The downstairs doors were open, and her brother's computer terminal was on. Max was nowhere in sight.

Reggie frowned, but she definitely felt more relaxed. Max was somewhere near her.

She closed her eyes for a moment, just because she was weary. Imagine! She had thought that she should go home.

She'd even thought that Wes might be worried.

Wes had never even gone home. Wes was here somewhere.

Wes . . . and Max.

What was it that no one was telling her?

The costume shop.

The idea entered unbidden into her mind. That's where Max was. She knew it, just as she sometimes knew that Max was in trouble. It had to do with their being twins, even if he was five minutes older.

She left the offices and started across the park for the costume shop. She glanced at her watch. It was nearly eleven o'clock. She'd had no idea that it had gotten so late. The cleaning crews had probably finished.

Still . . .

She suddenly had a very uneasy feeling as she moved through the empty park. Figures of dinosaurs that loomed big and friendly during the day seemed eerie and menacing in the dimmed, artificial light of the night.

The sound of her loafers against the cement walkways echoed with a chilling ring as she moved along.

"Max!" She meant to call his name out. Loudly.

It was little more than a croak.

She was glad a moment later.

For she heard another set of footsteps. They weren't loud against the pavement.

They were furtive. Someone was moving toward her. Toward the costume shop.

He or she was not using the pathways, but rather walking on the fringe of the foot roads, through the beautiful plants and shrubs.

Her heart quickened. Was she being followed? Or was someone else trying very hard not to be seen or heard?

She moved off the path and into the bushes. The costume shop loomed just ahead, the cave looking like a dark, squat opening to some strange pit.

In the night, it seemed to beckon.

Reggie bit her lip. She wondered if she shouldn't just call out, let it be known where she was and what she was doing.

No. She shouldn't give herself away to someone who hid in the darkness.

The darkness. The same darkness that frightened her had to be her protection. Wes had taught her that. An enemy couldn't fire at her in the darkness.

With renewed determination, she slipped off her shoes and started moving beside the path. Her footfalls made no sound.

She came around to the entry to the cave.

Then she realized that someone else was also embracing the darkness. Not a single light had been left on. Some illumination was always left.

Her breath coming very fast, Reggie fought the desire to leap for light, any light. She knew the costume shop.

Others might not.

Following the wall, she moved carefully past the rows of shelves and costuming. In another few minutes, she would be at the desk. The Victorian love seat and the chairs would be in front of the desk.

Who would be in the love seat tonight?

She flattened herself against the wall, her heart thundering. Why had she come here? What was she doing?

Max. Max was here.

Wasn't he?

Yes, someone was here. In the deadly darkness she could hear breathing, she could feel it. The place was silent, yet it was alive.

Then, suddenly, a voice burst out of the darkness. "Wes! Wes, where are you?"

Daphne's voice. Reggie felt ill. Daphne had set up a secret meeting with Wes. She was alive. It was all some kind of a con, and she was in it with Wes.

"Daphne, shut the hell up!" came Wes's voice in return.

Then Reggie knew exactly why he had warned Daphne. A shot rang out in the darkness, the flare at the gun's nose visible for a second.

From where she stood, near the desk, she realized that Daphne had been standing just beside it. She could hear movement. The gun was about to be fired again.

"Daphne, down!" Reggie shrieked out, and she took a flying leap for Daphne, encircling her with her arms, bearing her heavily to the ground.

She didn't know what had propelled her. She had never really liked her ex-sister-in-law, nor did she harbor any death wish of her own.

It just seemed like the thing to do at the moment.

She moved just in time. A second shot rang out. It grazed her temple, and for a moment, the world went black and spun. But she didn't pass out. She was aware almost instantly of a burning pain at the top of her head.

Then bedlam broke out. Someone was racing toward them, reaching for her. Daphne screamed.

Reggie managed to look up. A large shadow was looming over her.

Then just as suddenly, the shadow was gone.

There was a loud thudding sound from the center of the room. "Touch her, and you're dead!" she heard Wes call out.

Wes. Wes had called out those words.

Was he threatening anyone who might touch her . . . or anyone who might touch Daphne?

And then, at long last, the lights came on.

Reggie looked up.

Max was in one corner of the room, hurrying forward. Wes was on the floor, straddled over Rick Player.

Ozzie Daniels was standing just beyond Wes and Rick Player.

Daphne was beneath her. Reggie pulled her hand away from Daphne's shoulder in horror.

Blood was soaking her shoulder blade.

"Dear Lord!" Reggie exclaimed. "Someone call an ambulance, quickly. Daphne, Daphne—"

"Reggie! You're bleeding like a faucet yourself!" Wes exclaimed. He sounded furious. Was it anxiety, anger? And Max. Max had stepped forward and he looked pale.

What was going on? Who had fired the shot?

Rick was on the ground. Ozzie was by the door.

Max was carrying a gun. Wes, too, was carrying a gun. Oh, yes. The military man. The intelligence man. He would have a gun, and he would know how to use it. . . .

Reggie tried to stumble to her feet. "Get away from me, all of you!" she called out. She was sinking. She tried to pull Daphne up on her lap. She had to be breathing. She was. She could feel her ex-sister-in-law's heartbeat. "What the hell is going on here!" she cried out in panic.

There was another gun, Reggie saw suddenly. It was on the floor. It had been dropped in the midst of a scuffle.

Had Ozzie been carrying it? Or Rick?

Or did it matter?

Was the real danger facing her the man who had stolen her heart?

Wes's eyes met hers. They were a golden challenge. Did he condemn her for her fear of him, or simply dare her to interfere?

"Daphne, for the love of the God!" he whispered, low against her temple. "Daphne, you have to tell us who!"

Reggie could see Daphne's lips moving, but she couldn't hear what the woman was saying.

"Jesus!" Wes suddenly exploded, whirling around.

Rick Player was still on the ground, looking bruised and sick.

Ozzie Daniels was now the one with the power. His gun was in his hand. And it was aimed at Wes.

"I was right all along," Wes said, standing. "It was you. It was you, because you were holding some stock. And Daphne was foolish and bitter about her divorce. So if you could make the stock plummet, you thought you could seize control. And then you'd be avenged. Against Reggie—for refusing to find you attractive. Against Max—for hating everything that you stood for. But you didn't count on Daphne getting cold feet. When she did, when she wanted out, you decided to kill her. Only Daphne found out, and she was afraid of Max by then, afraid of everyone. And the poor woman believed that I could protect her. Damn it. Reggie, call an ambulance."

"If she makes a move to call anyone, you're dead," Ozzie said flatly.

"Screw this!" Max exploded. "One of us can rush him. He can't shoot both of us."

"But I can shoot Reggie," Ozzie said. "Ah, now that will give you both pause, won't it? Poor Daphne, there on the floor, her life's blood slipping away. I'm getting out of here. I'm not doing time for this. Reggie is coming with me, and if one of you moves a hair, she's dead. Reggie—oh, do excuse me, Miss Delaney.

You and your lousy crumbs of information. Get up. Get over here. Fast.''

"You sleaze!" Reggie said flatly. But she knew she was going. She still didn't understand about Wes and Daphne, but she didn't really care. She loved Max, and she loved Wes. She wasn't going to let either of them die.

"Reggie, don't do it!" Wes ordered.

But she was rising, ignoring his command.

"Come on, come on, faster!" Ozzie warned her.

"Oh, shut the hell up!" Reggie retorted. She was drawing his temper, she knew that. She didn't give a damn. He was walking toward her. He was going to wrench her into obedience.

But suddenly, he didn't.

A new voice called out. "Get him, Mr. Blake!"

And all of a sudden, Ozzie was tripping.

Wes didn't need a second invitation. He leaped forward and brought an arm sharply down on Ozzie's extended wrist.

Reggie heard a sickening crunch as bone broke.

Given a chance, Wes knew his business.

Ozzie's gun went clattering to the floor. And suddenly, standing before Reggie in the center of the floor was the little boy from the show that afternoon. The young man with the big blue eyes and the shaggy blond hair. He grinned broadly.

"We got him. We got him!"

"Yes, we got him," Wes agreed, retrieving Ozzie's gun from the floor. "But what are you doing here, young man!"

His voice was trembling. With fear, Reggie realized. For her, and for this boy.

"Who is this?" she asked.

"Joseph—" Wes began, but he broke off. They could all hear the sounds of sirens.

"It's Wiler," Max said to Wes.

"You managed to punch the alarm?" Wes said.

Max nodded. He started slowly toward Daphne, then knelt down beside her. Heedless of the blood at her shoulder, he lifted her into his arms.

Reggie bit her lip as she saw Daphne's beautiful eyes widen. "I'm sorry, Max," she whispered. "I don't know if you can believe me, but I'm sorry." Tears were filling her eyes.

Max nodded. "You're going to be all right, Daphne."

"It hurts like hell, Max."

"You've got a broken shoulder. But you're going to be okay."

"Promise?"

"Promise. I'm the magic man, remember? I can see that it's all right."

Reggie turned away from her brother's promise and stared at Wes. "She called me because she trusted me, and that was the only reason," he told her.

"But—"

"I told Max, but I didn't tell you, because I didn't want you here. Daphne wouldn't tell me anything over the phone. I didn't know who to be afraid of until I had seen her. I suspected Ozzie, because he had stock in the place. That's what I found out by working at the police station all those hours. It didn't make sense for a man who had stock in a place to make a scandal out of it. Unless he wanted stock prices to plunge. And that's just what he was trying for."

Yes, he had even told her so. He had just wanted her to think that Wes had been the one trying to do it.

"At first he was only trying to scare you, breaking into your house and firing shots at you. He forced Daphne to play the robotronic, and to try to scare you again in the park into doing something foolish. Then she wanted out. And he wanted her dead for real."

"How did he know that she was meeting you here tonight?" Reggie demanded. The sound of sirens was coming closer and closer.

He shook his head.

"I know!" Joseph announced.

Surprised, Reggie and Wes looked at him.

"You were supposed to be back at the home!" Wes told him sternly.

The boy grinned. "Well, you see, I just thought that you might need me. I told that nice Diana person that the home was sending a car for me. I pretended to run out to a white car, and then I slipped back."

"Precocious, isn't he?" Reggie said. She could almost smile.

"Brat!" Wes said warningly.

Joseph grinned. He pointed at Rick Player. "That man was hanging around when Diana called Mr. Delaney, and when Mr. Delaney said that he'd be tied up at the park with you, Wes, until very late."

Reggie spun around on Rick, who was not looking so rich or attractive, just very, very sick. "I had to know what was going on!" he said defensively.

"And you had to notify—Ozzie Daniels?" Reggie said incredulously.

"We've just got to buy his stock!" Wes said.

Then the doors burst open and Wiler, totally irritated, came through.

"All right, where do the explanations begin?"

"I need an ambulance for Daphne immediately!" Max said, standing angrily. "Then you can have all the explanations you want."

A stretcher was brought in for Daphne. Then a second arrived, and two paramedics with it stood patiently waiting in front of Reggie.

She looked at Wes. "Oh, no—"

"Oh, yes. You've got blood dripping down your forehead."

"But the bullet just grazed me!"

There was no protesting. He swept her off her feet and laid her out on the stretcher.

"But I'm not going to the hospital again!" she wailed.

A little hand suddenly slid into hers. "I think you'd better go, Reggie," Joseph told her solemnly. "You don't want to see Mr. Blake tonight. He really wants to tan your hide!"

"Oh, he does, does he?" Reggie exclaimed.

"I told him he should kiss you instead."

Neither suggestion mattered. The paramedics were taking her away.

"Wes—" she called.

But he wasn't with her. She closed her eyes and felt the wheels rumble over the concrete path.

It was over. Daphne was alive and, please God, she would remain so.

Max was in the clear.

And she had skirted terrible danger herself, and come out of it alive and fine.

So why did she feel so empty?

He had given her an explanation. At least, a bit of one. But he wasn't with her now.

She closed her eyes. He would come. He would come.

He didn't come. She was attended to by the same young physician who suggested she really should take better care of her head.

Wiler came, and she talked to him for at least thirty minutes.

Max came, and he told her that Daphne was going to be all right.

"I think she really did love you, Max," Reggie said.

"In her twisted way." He sighed. "I think we may be friends again. Never good friends, but the hatred is over."

"Isn't she going to have to face charges?"

"Not unless I press them. Or—unless you do."

Reggie shook her head.

"The doctor said you needed to sleep."

"Sleep! I'm going to get out of here. He's given me two stitches and—"

"He said he'll release you in time to do the show tomorrow afternoon."

"I can't! I have a breakfast appointment with Fran Rainier—"

"I'll keep it for you," Max promised. He caught hold of her shoulders and made her lie down. "Oh, Wes said that he'd talk to you tomorrow. Now good night. And Reggie—"

"Yes?"

"I love you. I thought I was going to die when Ozzie threatened you."

She smiled. "I love you, too, Max. We're twins."

He left her. She heard a clock ticking somewhere. Despite herself, giant tears welled in her eyes.

Last time she had been here, Wes had stayed, too. He had slept in the chair beside her.

Well, she had slapped him in the face.

He wanted to tan her hide, that was what Joseph had told her. But then, Joseph had told Wes that he should kiss her instead.

So which would it be?

She bolted up suddenly. Who was Joseph, anyway?

Max picked her up at the hospital and took her to the park just in time for the show. He was in an exceptionally good mood. He'd had another long talk with Daphne, he'd had a talk with Wiler in which he'd had the upper hand at last, and he'd had a great breakfast with Fran Rainier at the hotel.

"Fran will be at the show," he assured Reggie. "She's delighted with everything. She says you've given her a great vacation—and the exclusive of a lifetime!"

"That's nice," Reggie murmured. The whole world was happy.

Why did she feel so empty?

Bob, Stevie and Alise were all waiting for her with cheers and hugs when she came backstage to dress for the show. They demanded details, and she tried to explain everything.

Alise sighed. "And I thought it might be Rick Player."

"Naw, he's just a wimp," Bob decided. Reggie grinned.

Hindsight was always twenty-twenty.

They were being announced, there was no more time to talk. Within seconds she and Alise were running out on stage, fluffing their boas into the faces of their audience and bursting into song and dance. Soon Bob came along on his bucking stuffed bronco-saur, the bad guy, ready to shoot up the saloon. Then Stevie, the blond, blue-eyed hero showed up, ready to save the day.

Reggie went down the aisle, trying to decide whether to ride bucking dino-broncs with Bob and rob banks or to turn him into a man in the pursuit of good or evil. She played with various husbands and wives and children in the audience.

She started to stretch out a black-net-clad leg to climb up on the lap of the lean, jean-clad man sitting just behind the support beam.

She paused, her heart in her throat, then slamming there.

Wes was seated in that particular chair. And he was watching her, and his gold eyes were glittering.

She missed a beat.

"Howdy, stranger," she murmured.

She hadn't intended to sit on his lap.

Suddenly, she didn't have any choice. Strong arms were around her, pulling her down. "Howdy, stranger," he said in return.

She couldn't think of anything to say. Her throat was dry.

"Oh, Patricia, honey!" Bob called.

He was hot. So hot. She needed to escape.

She was in the middle of a show!

"What'd you find out there, Patricia?" Alise called out to her.

Damn. She'd been silent. Dead silent. In the middle of a show. With an entire audience watching her. Waiting.

She could feel the strength of his arms, the warmth of them. And she could see in his eyes everything that had been between them. Everything tempestuous and sensual and wild and fun . . .

And loving.

He smiled. A wicked, wicked smile.

She moistened her lips and flung her boa around his neck and pulled tight.

"Oh, I did find a live one out here, I did, I did!" she drawled to Alise.

There was a slight shifting in Wesley's legs. "Very much alive," he murmured huskily. "Very much."

The audience chuckled.

Bob hurried down the stairway.

"Patricia, honey. Remember me?"

She leaned forward, slipping her arms around Wes's neck, letting her eyes focus hugely on his. "What was that?"

The audience howled. Still . . .

They had played this scene before. Almost word for word.

"I said, I'm over here, honey!" Bob repeated. More laughter. "Excuse me, sir, would you?" He set a finger under Reggie's chin, turning her face to his. "Patricia, remember me?" He fell down on a knee before her. "Why, I'm going to cast aside my evil ways and make an honest woman out of you, honey! You're in love with me, honey—'scuse me, sir, your lap is in the way there! You've made an honest man of me, Patricia.''

"Oh, yes!" she exclaimed, blinking. "And your name was what . . . ?"

Again, the audience filled with laughter. It was probably one of the best shows they had ever done. It was killing her.

"Martin. Martin Van der Crime. Ah, excuse me, sir, she does have to marry me, sir."

"I do?"

"She does?"

"Yep. You can't have her, sir!"

"I can't?" Wes said. Another smile flickered across his features. "Why not?"

"'Cause I'm in this show, sir, and you're not!" Bob told him.

She liked the way Wesley laughed then. Good-naturedly. Willing to be part of the fun. Willing to believe in the magic.

But he shook his head firmly to Bob now. "Sorry, Bob. I can't let her marry you. Not this time around." Reggie's eyes widened with surprise. It was a show.

But Wes was rising, lifting her, then sitting her in his chair. And to her absolute amazement, he was on his knees before her.

"Reggie, you have to marry me. For real. Because I love you, and I need you. And because life is real itself, but so is that wonderful magic that you create. Will you marry me, Reggie?"

"But—"

"Joseph has said that he'll be delighted to be our son."

Her mouth fell open.

So that's who Joseph was!

And Joseph was there, next to Wes. She hadn't seen him at first because she had only been able to see Wes.

He was standing beside her then, too, that blond hair of his a wild mess in his eyes.

That was the first thing she was going to have to do. Get that boy—

No, her son. Her son!

She didn't know anything about him! But Wes wanted to marry her, and Wes had found him. And one look in his blue eyes and she knew—

Yes, first thing. She had to get her son a haircut.

"If you'll have me," Joseph said, clearing his throat. "I'll get good grades, I'll take out the trash, I'll do anything, honest, I promise."

Reggie started laughing. She hugged the little boy, pulling him close. "The trash doesn't matter!" she said. And she looked at Wes. "Love matters."

"Is that a yes?" he asked.

"Yes!"

There was a roar all around her. She had forgotten she was in the middle of a show until she heard that roar of approval.

Wes stood, sweeping her off her feet. He kissed her. Just like a prince kissing his Sleeping Beauty.

Again, the applause was thunderous.

Max was there, and Diana was with him. Bob and Stevie and Alise were rushing down the steps, then hugging her. Sweet little Alise. There were tears in her eyes.

Then someone spoke from the rear of the theater. "Now, this is an exclusive, Reggie Delaney! I just can't wait for it to hit the paper!"

She smiled beneath Wes's lips. Fran Rainier. Yes, the woman was getting her fill of stories!

Wes's lips rose from hers. "It's going to be front page news!" she warned him.

He nodded.

"Thank you!" she whispered.

"For the love?"

She grinned. "And the magic."

Holding her still, captured in the emerald of her eyes, he carried her out through the crowd and into the sunshine.

The day was clear and beautiful. Free from all evil.

Goodness had prevailed.

And they had their lives to plan.

Epilogue

Wes came tearing around the corner of the entranceway to Dierdre's DinoLand.

Reggie wasn't in her office—Max had already told him she wasn't. But she was in the park somewhere. And, Max assured him, she was tremendously anxious to see him. She could barely wait to see him.

Had she sensed that things would come to their conclusion today?

Knowing Reggie and the time, she was probably in costume as Dierdre, out playing with the children.

She might have gone to the lawyers with him, but he had dissuaded her from doing so. He hadn't been sure the paperwork would have all been completed.

And besides, Reggie had suddenly come up with a mysterious appointment of her own this morning. They had agreed to meet at the park.

He couldn't wait to see her.

His news was good. He couldn't wait to see her. He didn't care what she was doing—he just had to see her and let her know right away.

He burst into the courtyard where the big, human-sized dinosaurs were busy playing with the children.

Jeez. It was hard to tell one big stuffed pseudo-dino from another!

Ah . . . there was Dierdre, fluffing a little girl's hair, tickling a crying toddler and getting the little fellow to laugh.

It had to be Reggie. Only Reggie had that much patience.

He started toward her, then paused. Out of the corner of his eye, he could see another dinosaur appearing. Dolly Duckbill. He started quickly toward the creature, a smile suddenly curling his lip.

"Dolly!" He hoped it was someone he knew. "I'm Wes Blake. Do you know me?"

He heard soft laughter. "I most certainly do! And is your wife anxious to see you! She waited and waited in the costume shop, until just about two minutes ago."

It was Diana.

"Diana. I've just had great news. And I'd like a chance to tell Reggie in a special way. Can I have the costume?"

"This one won't fit you, but come on in and I'll get you a larger one. Quickly—before she sees us."

Diana took the duckbill mask and headpiece off as they entered the costume cave. She glanced at Wes, her eyes curiously alight. "You've got a surprise, huh?"

"A big one."

"About Joseph?"

He nodded. "The paperwork is through. He's ours. Free, clear, legally. His name is now Blake, and no one can ever take him away from us."

"That's wonderful!" Diana told him. She took a giant dinosaur head and the body to go with it from the rack in the shop and handed it to him. She stood on tiptoe and kissed his cheek. Her eyes were sparkling. "And how very interesting that it should be today..."

"What? Why's that?" Wes asked, grappling with the costume.

Diana shook her head. Wes realized that her eyes were sparkling. If he hadn't been quite so excited about Joe, he might have noticed earlier that she seemed to be amused and bemused, and that her eyes had been sparkling all along, as if she was a woman with some surprises of her own.

"Reggie will tell you, I'm sure," Diana said lightly. She patted his dinosaur head. "Enjoy! Oh, wait one minute!" She hurried across the shop and found a stuffed baby duckbill. The button eyes were huge, the lashes a mile long. "Think this might help?"

"I think it's great. But what—"

"Ciao! If you're here, I've got to run!"

Before he could question her again, Diana was gone.

Wes hurried into the Dino-Guys room and changed into the costume. With his stuffed toy held gingerly in his felt fingers, he lumbered out of the cave.

Children began descending on him. He patted heads, he awkwardly signed autographs.

He edged his way bit by bit closer to Reggie.

Bump!

He knocked her about a foot or so. Dierdre Dinosaur took a spin and stared at him. A little boy tugged on his arm. Wes turned and signed an autograph.

Bump!

Dierdre had given him a smack back. He spun, landing on his floppy green feet.

The children started to laugh delightedly.

He thought of Reggie behind that green mask, thought of the beautiful, giving woman. He thought of the love that she had given him, and he thought of how very much she had to share with children, and how she had ached for her own.

He lifted his hand, offering her the stuffed baby.

Slowly, slowly she reached out for it.

Dierdre wasn't supposed to talk.

Today, she did.

"Wes?"

He nodded. "Reggie, it's legal, it's all done. He's ours. Joe is ours. His name is Joseph Michael Blake, and he's—he's ours!"

"Wow! I never, never heard them talk out here before!" a little girl murmured.

Reggie was doing more than talking. She pulled off her Dierdre head, staring at him and then at the crowd. "Oh, Wes!" she exclaimed. Then she talked to the grown-ups and the children surrounding them. "Oh, I'm so sorry, excuse us, please! This is my husband, and we've just found out that we've legally adopted our little boy!"

A spatter of applause greeted her words. The crowd was in a good mood.

"It's Reggie Delaney!" someone said excitedly.

"Reggie Blake," Wes corrected. He winced, but Reggie hadn't minded. She was just giving him a crooked smile. Her eyes were alive and sparkling.

"Oh, Wes!"

He thought she was going to throw her arms around him, but she paused. "Oh, Wes!" Then, to his amazement, she reached behind her back.

She, too, was holding one of the baby duckbills.

"You knew?" he said, trying to understand why she had been carrying around a stuffed toy identical to his.

She shook her head. "No, no, I..." She hesitated. "I couldn't think of a good way to tell you. Wes, we're having our own, too. I didn't think that it was possible, but it is. I didn't want to say anything until I was really, truly sure, and the doctor had a cancellation this morning and I was able to see him. And you didn't act as if you wanted me to go to the attorneys with you—"

"I didn't want you to be disappointed if things weren't finalized and legal. Oh, Reggie, one of our own, too. Too, I mean two!" It was Wes's turn to look at the crowd. "I'm having two!" he announced with amazement.

Wes's announcement was greeted with another round of wild applause.

He pulled off his dinosaur head. He reached for her. He paused and spoke to the crowd. "Excuse me. I've just got to do this!"

Their costumes caused them to bump apart. He managed to pull her close anyway. He took her into his arms and soundly kissed her lips.

"Woah!" the little girl cried. "I've never, never seen them do this before!"

"It's all right," the girl's mother assured her. "They're just very excited. They're going to have babies."

"He's going to have a baby?" the girl inquired incredulously.

"No, no dear! Oh, never mind. I do think that the show is over."

"Heck, no!" a man called out. "Looks to me like the show's just beginning!"

"Harold!" his wife said sharply.

"Are they really going to have little dinosaurs?"

"No," the girl's mother said softly. "They'll have children—who maybe will grow up to create special dinosaurs and other characters."

Reggie broke from Wes, smiling at the woman's words. "Is that what we're going to have?"

"Who knows? But we'll definitely have a family. And I can guarantee that there's one thing we'll all create."

Her eyes were enchanting. Just a little moist. "Lots and lots of love!" she said.

He nodded. Once again he took her into his arms, to a clap of approval from the crowd. He held her chin with felt fingers and just brushed her lips with his kiss again.

"And magic," he told her. "Lots and lots—of magic!"

* * * * *

Ever since the appearance of Linda Howard's
incredibly popular MACKENZIE'S MOUNTAIN in 1989,
we've received literally hundreds of letters, all asking
that same question. At last the book we've all been
waiting for is here.

In September, look for MACKENZIE'S MISSION (Intimate
Moments #445), Joe's story as only Linda Howard
could tell it.

And Joe is only the first of an exciting breed here at
Silhouette Intimate Moments. Starting in September,
we'll be bringing you one title every month in our new
American Heroes program. In addition to Linda
Howard, the **American Heroes** lineup will be written
by such stars as Kathleen Eagle, Kathleen Korbel,
Patricia Gardner Evans, Marilyn Pappano, Heather
Graham Pozzessere and more. Don't miss a
single one!

Welcome to Conard County, Wyoming, where the sky spreads bold and blue above men and women who draw their strength from the wild western land and from the bonds of the love they share.

Join author Rachel Lee for a trip to the American West as we all want it to be. In Conard County, Wyoming, she's created a special place where men are men and women are more than a match for them.

In the first book of the miniseries, EXILE'S END (Intimate Moments #449), you'll meet Amanda Grant, whose imagination takes her to worlds of wizards and warlocks in the books she writes, but whose everyday life is gray and forlorn—until Ransom Laird walks onto her land with trouble in his wake and a promise in his heart. Once you meet them, you won't want to stop reading. And once you've finished the book, you'll be looking forward to all the others in the miniseries, starting with CHEROKEE THUNDER, available in December.

EXILE'S END is available this September, only from Silhouette Intimate Moments.

**It's Opening Night in October—
and you're invited!
Take a look at romance with a
brand-new twist, as the stars
of tomorrow make their
debut today!
It's LOVE:
an age-old story—
now, with
*WORLD PREMIERE
APPEARANCES* by:**

Patricia Thayer—Silhouette Romance #895
JUST MAGGIE—Meet the Texas rancher who wins this pretty
teacher's heart...and lose your own heart, too!

Anne Marie Winston—Silhouette Desire #742
BEST KEPT SECRETS—Join old lovers reunited and see what
secret wonders have been hiding...beneath the flames!

Sierra Rydell—Silhouette Special Edition #772
ON MIDDLE GROUND—Drift toward Twilight, Alaska, with this
widowed mother and collide—heart first—into body heat
enough to melt the frozen tundra!

Kate Carlton—Silhouette Intimate Moments #454
KIDNAPPED!—Dare to look on as a timid wallflower blos-
soms and falls in fearless love—with her gruff, mysterious
kidnapper!

**Don't miss the classics of tomorrow—
premiering today—only from**

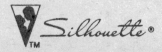

PREM